GOPAL'S GULLY

Read more for middle-grade readers from Duckbill

Ninja Nani and the Bumbling Burglars by Lavanya Karthik
Ninja Nani and the Mixed by Lavanya Karthik
Ninja Nani and the Zapped Zombie Kids by Lavanya Karthik
Against All Odds by Ramendra Kumar
The Case of the Candy Bandit by Archit Taneja
The Case of the Careless Aliens by Archit Taneja
Oops the Mighty Gurgle by RamG Vallath
The Deadly Royal Recipe by Ranjit Lal
Vanamala and the Cephalopod by Shalini Srinivasan
Flat-track Bullies by Balaji Venkataramanan
Pops! by Balaji Venkataramanan
Ravana Refuses to Die by Rustom Dadachanji
Dhanak by Anushka Ravishankar and Nagesh Kukunoor
Simply Nanju by Zainab Sulaiman
Hot Chocolate is Thicker than Blood by Rupa Gulab
The Sherlock Holmes Connection by Martin Widmark, Anushka Ravishankar, Katarina Genar and Bikram Ghosh
Tiger Boy by Mitali Perkins
The Hill School Girls: Alone by A. Coven
The Hill School Girls: Secrets by A. Coven
The Hill School Girls: Strangers by A. Coven
The Hill School Girls: Trouble by A. Coven
Karma Fights a Monster by Evan Purcell
Karma Meets a Zombie by Evan Purcell
Karma vs the Evil Twin by Evan Purcell
The Piano by Nandita Basu

GOPAL'S GULLY

Zarin Virji

duckbill

An imprint of Penguin Random House

DUCKBILL BOOKS

USA | Canada | UK | Ireland | Australia
New Zealand | India | South Africa | China

Duckbill Books is part of the Penguin Random House group of companies whose addresses can be found at global.penguinrandomhouse.com

Published by Penguin Random House India Pvt. Ltd
4th Floor, Capital Tower 1, MG Road,
Gurugram 122 002, Haryana, India

Penguin Random House India

First published in Duckbill Books by
Penguin Random House India 2021

10 9 8 7 6 5 4 3 2

ISBN 9780143451907

Typeset in Josefin Sans by PrePSol Enterprises Pvt. Ltd

Printed at Repro India Limited

www.penguin.co.in

FSC www.fsc.org
MIX
Paper from responsible sources
FSC® C047271

1

We reached Mumbai late in the evening. I was tired, hot and sweaty. What else to expect at the beginning of March?

Watching the double-decker buses, the cars, the small black and yellow taxis was fascinating, but the noise was deafening. Such intense sounds! And the smell—I didn't know what it was but it was foul.

We walked on and on forever. My headache got worse. When Sanjiv Maama said we had reached home, I stared hard.

We were on a narrow road with a green wall on one side. There were houses across the road, but on the side where we were was just one long stretch of wall. There was a rickety wooden ladder placed against it. Not saying a word, he climbed up the ladder and I followed him, to walk down a similar ladder on the other side. Next to this ladder stood a tin shack alongside the railway tracks. This was home?

Not that home earlier had been a palace; my village home was a half-pukka, half-kutcha house.

The kutcha part housed the two goats and the fowls while we had a kitchen and three rooms in the pukka section. There was never enough money, neither for the windows to be fitted nor for the plastering; with every passing monsoon, the structure worsened, becoming more and more derelict.

The villagers said I was unfortunate. They pitied me. Poor boy, his father's dead and now his mother's gone too. I didn't really mind. Amma used to thrash me quite often for no reason. Then she'd sit and cry for hours after her chores were done.

My father, 'the alcoholic brute' in Amma's words, died when I was barely two; her in-laws decided to get rid of her for 'eating up' her husband, so her father, Baba, was summoned to take her away. That's how we ended up in Badriya.

For ten years, Amma slaved in the small plot of land behind our house. Her job was to see to the sowing and harvesting of maize and pulses while Baba worked in the zamindar's sugar cane fields. By the time I was seven, I started helping with the odd jobs in the zamindar's haveli; Baba said that would help us to wipe off our debts.

Amma's health was always frail, but it was her cough that did her in. It accompanied her wherever she went. Before Diwali last year, her cough worsened. Neither the medicine from the government health centre nor the smoke-and-broom routine from the witch doctor helped.

When she began spewing out blood four months later, everyone was convinced that she'd die sooner rather than later.

It did feel strange to see her lying cold and silent and then being carried away. And worst of all, I had to light the funeral pyre and get my head shaved.

But at the back of my mind was this growing anticipation—Sanjiv Maama was taking me to Mumbai! I was almost thirteen, and I was more than ready to get away. Sanjiv Maama used to boast about Mumbai being a charmed city of tall buildings swarming with movie stars. And I'd finally get to see the sea!

Amma dying didn't feel so bad, after all.

I wasn't fond of Sanjiv Maama. No sane person could really like a short-fused guy such as him. But what did it matter? At least he agreed to have me tag along.

Actually, it was because Baba convinced him that I could add to the family income by finding a job of some sort. To earn my own money sounded exciting in itself, but also because I would no longer have to deal with my bossy aunt and her non-stop orders and her three little squealing children. I'd also be able to rid myself of the label 'Gopal, the low-caste boy' as nobody bothered about caste in Mumbai according to Sanjiv Maama.

My excitement about the journey evaporated almost as soon as our travels began. I could not stop retching from the time we left our village at noon on a rattling bus. We reached Lakhimpur as the sun was setting, because a tyre burst. I was left idling at the railway station while Sanjiv Maama went off to pass the better part of the night with his friends. Like a spineless scarecrow, my body crumpled on the railway bench, too tired to take in the goings-on at the station.

Even before the roosters began to crow, Sanjiv Maama shook me awake to board the train to Lucknow. After another long wait at Lucknow, we were finally on our way to Mumbai in the Gorakhpur Express.

All the seats were already filled with twice or thrice the number of passengers that could be accommodated, so we settled ourselves on the floor near the toilets. The men all lit their bidis after every meal. The smoke made my eyes tear and made me cough. Was I glad when the disgusting journey came to an end!

But it seemed trains were going to be a part of my home now. Just as I entered the shack, two trains from opposite ends went past each other. One hooted to welcome me.

Sanjiv Maama left to get us something to eat.

There was one more shack a short distance away, and a leafy canopy shaded both these dwellings. This tree was unlike the trees in our village; it had pink blossoms with small green leaves. The greyish orange sky was peeping through its umbrella-shaped crown. The tree was rooted on the other side of the wall, next to the street.

I scaled the wall to check out the tree and dropped down on the other side. Just as I had hoped, I could easily climb up and down this tree. While I was wondering whether to explore the tree now or the next day, a ball rolled to the foot of the ladder.

'Hey, you there, throw it back!'

I glanced across the road. Two boys, around my age, were playing cricket.

I smiled and threw it back. They resumed their game. Forget calling me to join them, they didn't even acknowledge me after getting their ball back.

I had to scale the tree then and there to let them see how good I was at climbing. I clambered up swiftly. The leaves brushing against my skin felt so cool. Resting my head against the fork of the boughs, I was reminded of the games in our basti. We played lagori and gilli danda, while the zamindar's folk mostly played cricket. When Masterji wanted to take a nap, he let us play langdi taang.

'Gopal, what are you doing? Are you going to trouble me like this? Come down and eat.'

That was my loving Sanjiv Maama. Better to listen to him so that he wouldn't find a reason to send me back. When he'd go to work, I could do whatever I wanted.

I went down meekly and took some stuff wrapped in newspaper from him.

'What's this?'

'Don't ask questions. I'm tired. It's vada pav. Most famous dish in Malad. Not just Malad, all over Mumbai.'

He was silent while he chomped on his portion.

And then, as if he had been thinking, he continued, 'How in hell am I going to find a job for you? Skills, you have none. And forget becoming a hero; with your looks you won't even make it as a Bollywood extra. What a sorry package you are—scrawny legs, owlish eyes and rabbit teeth!'

'Baba says I have a good memory!' I said in my own defence.

'That's because you have nothing better to do. You just loiter and watch people and remember word for word what people say. Nobody's going to pay you any money for that!'

He frowned and wiped his hands on the newspaper and threw it away. Then he lit a bidi and squatted on the doorstep of the shack with his back towards me. I could have told him that he didn't look much better himself with his potato-nose, but I held my tongue.

The breeze was great, but the rumbling of trains was unbearable. I stuffed the bed sheet into my ears to muffle the noise, but it didn't help much. Gradually, I must have fallen asleep from the exhaustion.

That's how my first day in Mumbai ended.

2

When my eyes opened, Sanjiv Maama was getting ready to go to work. The machine tools factory where he worked was close by.

'Where do I go, you know, for the early morning stuff . . . ?' I asked, putting my little finger up.

'Go anywhere,' he sniggered. He pointed to the railway tracks. 'All this is our toilet. Just don't get your thing cut off.'

I selected a spot behind a bush. Just right. Others came by for the same purpose, some carrying buckets of water, some bringing umbrellas to shield their faces.

Trains kept coming from both directions, every three-four minutes, packed with commuters. It was different from squatting in the fields; except for the occasional animal, I was pretty much on my own when I went for the big job in my village.

I went back home and washed up. I ate the remnants of last night's meal with some tea. No sugar, no milk. Sanjiv Maama had said he would ask for an advance from his employer and stock the kitchen with some essentials this evening.

Then I was over the wall in a jiffy. I had nothing to do and a whole day in which to do it.

I scanned the street. The wall separating it from the tracks ran along one side. The other side was a row of ground-plus-one pukka structures, painted green and blue, pink and grey. Each one fitted with an iron staircase leading to the first floor. At this hour, there were children going off to school and men to work.

I walked a short while to the left until I came to a mountain of garbage. The stench made me turn back and walk quickly in the other direction.

After a bit, the row of one-storeyed houses became taller buildings. Must be for the rich folk.

I did not want to wander too far on my first day. I turned to go back. And that's when I saw her.

She was leaning over the first floor balcony of her house. While she was unlike any girl I had seen before, she reminded me of a story I had heard. The zamindar's wife used to put her two-year-old to bed by telling him stories. My favourite one—I don't know why—was about a pari, whose skin was as fair as milk and whose eyes were brown and soft like a deer's. And she had a laugh that sounded like a bell. I had liked the description, though I had also thought it was silly.

But this girl looked like she had stepped out from that story.

I turned my gaze away, but it was too late. She had caught me gawking at her.

'Who are you? I have never seen you before,' she demanded.

I pretended not to have heard her.

'Don't you have a tongue? What's your name?'

'Gopal,' I said, looking down.

'What kind of name is that?'

'The one given by my baba.'

She laughed. And her laughter was indeed like the chime of a bell, clear and joyful.

I felt my face going red. I took a few steps in the direction I had to go.

'Hey,' she said, 'I haven't finished talking! Walking away like that!' She laughed again.

I stood transfixed. I didn't know what to do next.

'I'm unwell, so I didn't go to school. I was getting bored, so I came out here. I need someone to talk to, no? I'm Aisha.'

I simply nodded because I didn't know what to say.

'Don't you go to school?'

'Yes, no, no,' I sputtered.

'What do you mean? Look here!'

I looked at her and felt myself going red again.

'You are new around here, aren't you? Where have you come from?'

'Badriya village, Lakhimpur Kheri district, Uttar Pradesh.'

Each word fell on the one before and came out in a rush. My gaze snapped back to the area around my feet.

'Come inside, Aisha. Your fever will return unless you lie down,' called a voice from inside the house.

'Coming, Nani,' she replied quickly.

I stole a glance in her direction.

'Now I have to go in and I still haven't got to know you!' She stuck her tongue out at me and waved before disappearing.

I looked fixedly at the balcony. Did she want to befriend me? I couldn't work it out.

As I walked back to the shack, I wished I could go back home. I didn't know anyone here. In that moment, I even missed my stupid aunt.

I climbed the tree and buried my face amid its leaves, sobbing quietly.

After a bit, low yelps, similar to the sound in my throat, drew my attention. It was a three-legged mongrel looking up at me hopefully. I climbed down to pat him. His barks grew more and more plaintive, and he wagged his tail. He licked my hands hungrily while I dug deeper into his dirt-brown fur. Then, after a bit, he settled down for a nap.

My gaze moved westwards. Beyond the tracks were clusters of tall buildings. I could not tell how many floors in each. I decided to count. I began with the ugly grey one on the left—six floors. Then the yellow-brown one—that one was ten. And the blue-white one that jutted out was twenty floors or more. Exhausted by the squinting and counting, I fell asleep.

When I awoke, the dog was nowhere in sight. The sun was almost overhead; I must have been asleep a good two hours.

I set off, past the garbage heap, to search for my new friend. When I looked up, I realized there was a road going above my head. This Mumbai was truly magical, with a surprise wherever I turned.

I was glad I walked down that way because it was such a lively place with small shops in almost each tenement. A chicken shop sat next to a ladies' tailor. Mouth-watering food smells wafted out of another shop—they were making biryani. There were big pots on the veranda. Another man was selling biscuits and cigarettes, and next to that was a barber's shop. Further on was a bicycle repair shop.

The old man from the bicycle shop called me towards him. He was dressed in a white kurta and pyjamas.

'You, come here! Aren't you Sanjiv's nephew? Come, beta, sit.'

I sat on the stool he pushed towards me.

'I have lived in Squatters Colony gully for so long that I know everyone around here. You looked new and lost, so I put two and two together.' He chuckled, stroking his beard. He had a mole near his left eye.

My eyes took in his shop. A wooden rack with various tools stood against one wall while the other had tyres of different sizes hanging off pegs. The pump was placed against the third wall.

'You must be missing your village. We all do. I still remember my first day in this city. That was forty long years ago. I came from Ratnagiri, which is in Maharashtra only, but still everything was so different. You've come all the way from UP! Slowly-slowly you'll get used to this city.' He let out a big sigh.

'Abdul Chacha, quick, change for Rs 500,' said a passer-by.

'Haan, haan, let me see what I have.' Abdul Chacha unlocked a drawer beneath the shelves stacked with cardboard boxes and counted out the notes before handing them to the man-in-a-hurry.

'Have you had lunch, Gopal?' asked Abdul Chacha.

'No, I'm not hungry,' I lied. The aroma of the biryani was making my stomach growl.

'Son, it's time for me to eat, so you can give me company, no?'

I nodded.

A curtain separated the shop from his house. He went in for a moment and soon a young woman brought us two steel plates with dal, rice and mango pickle. She was Sana, his daughter-in-law who was a big support, he said, while his son, Jamir, was away working in Qatar. She smiled shyly.

I ate heartily—my first home-cooked meal in three days! Abdul Chacha called out for a second helping of rice.

A voice from inside yelled that he was supposed to watch his diet.

'My wife,' he whispered to me with another wink. 'Very strict, because I have diabetes.'

He took me behind the shop to the front room of his house so that I could wash my hands and drink some water. Two blue drums for water storage dwarfed everything else in the room, but I also noticed there was a gas stove on the kitchen counter and a refrigerator beside the TV cabinet. Behind yet another half-drawn curtain, I could make out another room with a bed and a steel cupboard, and there were stairs leading to the floor above.

Sana, who had brought us food, and an older woman, who must have been Abdul Chacha's wife, were both sitting on the floor eating their meal. They covered their heads with their dupattas when they saw us.

Abdul Chacha asked me to mind the shop while he went in for a nap. Slightly panicked, I said I wouldn't know what to do if a customer came along. Patting me on the head, he told me to wake him up if someone did as he vanished inside.

I sat there for who knew how long, watching the motorbikes, tempos and cars go by. Little children were riding their bicycles, some were playing with a bat and a ball, fearlessly in the middle of that road. Not a single person came to disturb me.

When Abdul Chacha returned, he looked refreshed. He combed his hair and his beard and peered at me through his glasses.

'Shabaash, beta. Let's have some tea. Then you run along.'

'Can I stay here, I mean, can I help with something?'

'Why not?'

Soon people started streaming in—mostly children who needed to get air pumped into the tyres. Chacha really knew everyone. And the good thing was that he introduced me to all those who came.

A young man with bulging biceps and a saffron tilak offered me a spin 'double-seated' on his cycle. I looked towards Chacha for approval, but he merely shrugged his shoulders. I took that to mean it was fine.

Raja rode quite rashly, going very close to all the cars, giving me a scare. I was also used to riding fast, but that was in Badriya where I didn't have to watch out for cars or trucks, just the occasional motorbike. Raja careered past the tenements, past the buildings and swerved left on to the bigger and busier road.

At the edge of this road stood a park where Raja halted and parked his cycle near the gate. He took me in to meet his friends.

There was a banyan tree at the far end of the park that spread its branches over most of it. There were four neat squares of soft green grass skirted with multicoloured flowering bushes. The park was gorgeous, but Raja's friends seemed like trouble, not my type at all.

I had seen two of them yesterday—the boys whose ball I had thrown back. Their names were Yakub and Imtiaz and they did not seem to recognize me.

What made me very happy was that the dog from the morning was also there. When he came towards us wagging his tail, the boys shouted, 'Tiger, come here,' and tossed some candy wrappers at him. Tiger sniffed hopefully and then moved aside, his tail drooping. His action made the boys double up with laughter.

Raja slapped one or two boys and then whistled to Tiger as he threw an empty cigarette pack at him. Tiger looked away disinterestedly, making one of the younger boys go and tug at his tail as though he were milking a cow. Tiger yelped in pain and shuffled away, as far as his three legs could carry him. The boys howled uproariously as Raja mimicked the dog's gait.

Losing interest in the animal, they started playing cards and asked me to join them. I excused myself saying Sanjiv Maama would be home soon and I needed to be back.

As I was trying to find my way back, the clanging of bells and chanting took my eyes to a gated enclosure. Must be a temple of some sort, but exploring it could wait till tomorrow. I made my way back to the shack and watched the local trains going by, astonished that no one fell out as so many were crammed in the doorway of each compartment.

When Sanjiv Maama finally got home with a small bag of groceries, I was pleased to see him.

He may not have been the greatest of guys, but he was all I could call my own in this city.

'Can you make roti?' he asked.

I said that I could not. Cooking was something Amma and my aunt did.

'I don't know how long I can put up with you! Here, watch how I do it so that you can take over,' he said gruffly as he added water to the flour and slapped the dough around.

'Don't forget, keeping the shack clean and fetching water is your responsibility from tomorrow.'

I nodded as I peeled the potatoes for the sabji.

'The good thing is that Abdul Chacha has taken a fancy to you. He may be a Muslim, but he's a decent chap. He wants you to work for him. He'll pay Rs 20 per day with lunch and tea. Not bad for a useless fellow like you.' He laughed as he rolled out the rotis and hurled them on the tawa.

'Really?' My eyes began to dance. 'When do I start?'

'Tomorrow, of course! And mind you, no goofing off. Chacha's shop is open seven days a week.'

That night I couldn't fall asleep. A similar excitement used to creep up on me whenever we went to the mela ground at Lakhimpur for the Ramlila festival. Maybe Mumbai wasn't such a bad place.

3

The mullah's call for prayers awakened me and then sleep was out of the question.

My first day at work! I'd better be early. I would wear the red striped shirt to mark this day. My other three shirts and three half pants were hand-me-downs from the zamindar's middle son. But this red one was brand new since it had been given to me for the thirteenth-day ceremony after Amma's death.

As soon as Sanjiv Maama left, I set myself to tidying the shack. I placed the bedding and Primus stove outdoors while I swept the mud floor. As our trunks were chained to the wooden pole, I could only sweep around them. The water drum was too heavy to be moved. I dusted the rack that held the pots. Finally, I brought back in the objects I had placed outside and pushed them back into position. I whistled as I went about my ablutions, dressing quickly.

Galloping away past the rubbish heap, I was trying to run faster than the trains whizzing past when I was halted by a monstrous truck flying straight at me.

'Who do you think you are? Running in the middle of the road?' the driver bellowed. 'Do you have a death wish or something? Move aside!'

I hurried past the green monster before the driver could say anything more. A foul rotten stench was coming from its belly. Two men were hanging over its back, laughing.

I crossed the road and turned to look back.

The truck stopped by the rubbish heap. The two men jumped off, scooped up part of the rubbish and the beast roared off. Why didn't they take away all the garbage piled up?

I walked on towards the cycle shop.

No sign of Chacha. Should I go in? No, that would look as if I was overeager. Better to wait.

I crossed the street and leaned on a motorbike that was parked there.

'Hey, what are you doing here? Just hanging around the neighbourhood, eh?'

The voice made me lose my balance and I stumbled off the bike. The bell-like laughter followed.

It was the pari. She was accompanied by two other girls, all dressed for school in pale blue checked kameezes, white salwars and white dupattas.

'No, I work here,' I said and pointed towards the cycle shop.

'Work?' she said, screwing up her nose. 'That means you don't go to school? You're illiterate, aren't you?'

'No,' I said, 'I can read and write. And count.'

'Shabaash,' she said, clapping her hands. 'Even Nani can do that much. And that's enough for you?' Her plaits bobbed up and down with every word she spoke.

Chacha's appearance in the shop saved me from further humiliation.

'I have to go now.'

I scurried across the street to my new refuge.

Abdul Chacha greeted me warmly. I cast a glance behind me to see if the girls had gone away. Chacha caught me staring at her.

'You want to go to school, don't you, beta?' he asked kindly.

'No, no, not at all,' I said, shaking my head. 'I want to work.'

'We all say that, don't we, when the grapes are sour . . .' He patted my head.

I didn't understand what he meant, but I nodded.

'Your uncle of course doesn't earn much and he has to send money home, poor chap. So you cannot have the luxury of going to school,' he said with a deep sigh. 'Chalo, let's do the best we can. Arre, Sana, come here,' he shouted.

Sana emerged, wearing a polka-dotted pink and white salwar kameez. She pulled her dupatta closer to her forehead.

'Gopal, my daughter-in-law is a very hard-working girl. Her day begins at four in the morning, when the municipal water is supplied. After that she goes about doing countless household chores before giving tuitions to the colony children in the evenings.'

He turned to his daughter-in-law. 'Sana beta, why don't you make him sit with you when your students come? That way Gopal will also learn something.'

'As you wish, Abbaji.' Two deep dimples formed in her cheeks when she smiled. She turned to go back inside.

Panic hit me. School didn't mean anything to me. In fact, I had hated it—why should I torture myself again?

'I just want to work with you,' I said, touching his feet.

'So you are not fond of books, badmaash!' Chacha said with a laugh. 'Books have knowledge and knowledge makes us wise. If you want to work here, you will have to study.' Sternness had entered his voice.

I nodded. I really liked this man and I didn't want to lose my job.

'Now go and give this parcel at the mosque,' he said, pointing to a structure two or three tenements away.

I didn't know there was a mosque in the vicinity. I went and knocked at the door. Luckily, I didn't have to say anything. The man who opened the door took the parcel from my hands with a nod. I came back promptly.

Chacha didn't have too many customers that day. I hoped more people would come so that he would continue to let me work for him. I was told to arrange the screws size-wise in boxes on the shelves and dust the shelves. Work made me happy. I wasn't a kaamchor at all.

Chacha left for the mosque for his afternoon prayers. Sana came out asking me if I had gone to school at all. I said yes, I had studied till Class V. Then she asked if I knew English. I shook my head.

'At least your Hindi must be strong. You can be my assistant tutor,' she said as she turned to go in. Was that some kind of joke?

With Chacha's return, our lunch arrived. It was a brinjal sabji, roti and tiny fried fish full of bones. At home I wouldn't have eaten brinjal, but in

Chacha's presence I couldn't turn it down. I refused the second helping politely.

When Chacha retired for his nap, Sana brought a Class V Hindi Reader and asked me to read aloud. I read somewhat shyly at first and then with greater confidence when I noticed her approving nods.

'You're good, Gopal.' She smiled. *If you think I'm 'good', you are weird, Sana,* I thought.

About ten children of various shapes and sizes, younger than I was, came at five o'clock, dragging their school bags. Sana called me inside and proceeded to make the introductions. We all sat on the floor in a circle. She called each child to her, asked what homework they'd been given and helped each one begin.

Seven-year-old Rizwan was struggling with maths. I solved the sums for him quickly to impress Sana. She gave me a broad smile. Impish Sameera inched closer to me and gave me her book—maths again. Once again I solved the problems, earning me another smile from Sana.

When the children left, it was seven o'clock. I had had no idea that so much time had elapsed. In the village school, we used to wait for the school gong to be sounded, signalling the end of the day.

I got up to leave after thanking Sana. She laughed because I addressed her as 'teacherji'.

She said it was too formal and that I call her Bhabhi instead.

She followed me out and asked me to wait. Chacha was dealing with a customer.

When the customer left, Bhabhi said, 'Gopal is very good at maths, Abbaji. He can help you with the accounts.'

My ears turned beet red on hearing so much praise, all in one day!

'Wah, Gopal! You will be quite an asset to me,' he said, pushing up the glasses on his nose.

I mumbled my thanks as I left. I used to keep the accounts at home too, writing the daily expenditure in Baba's diary. So does everybody, I'm sure. This family was abnormal . . . in a nice way, of course. I hoped they would remain the same. For now I should better hurry back to my home.

I quickened my steps, almost running past the stinking garbage spot. And then remembered that Sanjiv Maama was going to a friend's, so he would come by nine o'clock. What should I do now?

I took the long flight of stairs to the road going above my head. For a while, I stood there mesmerized, watching the vehicles crawling past. Why did people sit in those cars and buses? Surely they would travel faster if they walked or cycled. The rows of autorickshaws looked like an army of cockroaches coming to invade the city.

There were so many different kinds of people in the city. They looked different, talked differently, dressed differently. I had never seen so many kinds of people in all my life before coming to Mumbai.

After a while, the sound and the fumes began to give me a headache. As I hurried down the steps, I heard the ringing of the bells once again.

Would this temple be open to SCs? In our parts, we dared not go near certain temples; they were strictly off limits for my people. But here nobody knew me, so I ventured towards it bravely as the sounds grew louder.

My timing was perfect. The aarti was on and that meant prasad would surely follow. I stood behind a small group and clapped my hands to the beat of the cymbals. The language of the song was unfamiliar, but I didn't mind.

As soon as it ended, a fat lady wearing lots of gold muttered something in her language and everyone moved to one side and sat down in a row. I thought I'd better leave, but the lady gestured to me. Had I done something wrong? Switching to Hindi, she ordered me to sit with the others. I did as she told.

A boy placed banana leaves in front of each worshipper followed by another who served halwa, pickle and papad on our banana-leaf plates. Then the first one reappeared with sabji, and the second one brought rice and dal. As we ate, they kept offering us more.

The stern lady walked up and down. She asked me where I lived and what I did. When I told her, she looked at me pityingly. She said I could come daily for my evening meal. I folded my hands to thank her.

As people finished eating, the crowd thinned out. I washed my hands and walked towards the gate.

I spied Raja ushering a delicate young woman towards the pujari. From the corner of my eye, I watched as he whispered something to the pujari, then both he and the girl bent down to touch the man's feet. The pujari handed them the customary flowers and coconut slivers before turning away to perform the ritual of putting the gods to bed.

I was satisfied with how the day had turned out. Mumbai was treating me like a prince! I could see why everyone from our village longed to migrate to this city.

4

I was approaching the pile of trash when the garbage truck thundered to a stop and the driver waved to me. Not knowing whether to return his greeting or not, I carried on; I did not want him to start yelling at me again.

I described my visit to the temple to Chacha. He said it was an ashram set up by Maharashtrians. That explained the strange language. Chacha suggested that I could go to the ashram daily for the evening meal and prayers. I told him that the gods in there being Marathi-speaking wouldn't be of much use to me.

Chacha laughed and said, 'God is one, Gopal. And he knows all languages. He understands our needs, even the unspoken ones. All we need to do is believe in him.'

This didn't make any sense to me. Whenever Amma used to beat me, I had prayed to god to protect me, but god never did.

As soon as Chacha left for the mosque, Bhabhi, who was coughing, came out to chat with me.

Chachi was resting, she said. She had had the viral fever that was sweeping through the colony for the past two days. She was weak and had lost her appetite.

Bhabhi said, 'You must go back to school, Gopal. The new academic year will soon begin and Abbaji can help with your admission.'

'No need. I'm quite happy working here.'

'What about your future?' she said.

I looked away.

She continued, 'Education is important, Gopal. Take my case. Because I have done my BA, I can give tuitions, don't you see?'

I didn't want to offend her so I nodded, but I was mighty impressed. In our village only a few men were BA pass. You had to go to the city to study further.

'I know funds are a problem,' she said, 'but schooling is free and some other costs your uncle can surely bear.'

She was obviously clueless about Sanjiv Maama. I kept nodding.

I knew Sanjiv Maama barely made enough for himself and to send home. I knew I was a burden to the family as I didn't have parents. School was not for me. Anyway, what did it matter? Sanjiv Maama had never been to school, neither had Amma.

Bhabhi went back into the kitchen. I followed her determined to ask her the question that was nagging me.

'How far is the sea from here?'

'Not so far,' she said.

When I told her that I had never, ever seen the ocean, Bhabhi promised that she would take me there some day. Then she gave me a slight push to go and mind the shop.

Through a crack between the curtain and the wall, I saw her put on her earphones and fiddle with her mobile phone as she pulled out a giant bundle of dupattas from a cupboard.

I leant in and asked, 'Why do you have so many dupattas?'

'The ladies in the colony like our handwork, so Ammiji and I do embroidery, crochet and lacework on these dupattas.'

'Why have you taken on this additional work, Bhabhi? Jamirbhai is anyway working hard and sending all his income home.'

Her dimples deepened. 'Gopal, your bhai's salary goes towards the loan for the construction of the first floor room and EMIs towards the fridge and TV. Besides, I like doing this.'

I watched her fingers nimbly sewing a purple lace to a yellow dupatta and later sticking some sparkling electric-blue sequins to a pink one. Whenever one of her favourite songs was playing, she sang along tunelessly, tapping her feet or jiggling her shoulders, in spite of the irritation in her throat.

The afternoon got busier. Chacha sent me off to fetch some tools. His instructions were clear, so I made it to the shop easily. My sense of direction was pretty good and I wasn't worried about how I would find my way back.

'Gopal, Gopal!'

I stopped to look back, wondering who was calling my name.

It was Raja on a motorbike, gleaming black and red metal.

'Chal, aaja! Are you headed to the shop?'

I nodded and he offered to drop me back.

'Is this motorbike yours? It must be very expensive,' I asked as I got off, touching its engine reverentially.

'How does it matter? It's mine whenever I want to ride it.' He laughed, sliding his hand over the back seat. He pushed off with a big roar.

That evening I couldn't join Bhabhi's tuition class as customers kept us on our toes. Sameera was told off for slipping her notebook to me several times to get some multiplication problems solved.

I was peeing by the tracks when a gruff voice called out, 'You are under arrest!'

I zipped up hastily and turned to face a middle-aged woman with straggly hair, her sari hitched up almost to her knees.

'Haven't you heard about the fine for soiling rail property?'

She threw her head back and laughed on seeing my panic-stricken face. 'Relax,' she said. 'I didn't mean to startle you!'

She was walking daintily along the tracks, picking up the rubbish from the coarse stones under the tracks and throwing it into one of two bags.

'What are you doing here?' I asked.

'Don't mind me. I'm just a woman doing her job,' she said with a twinkle in her eye and that hoarse laugh.

'Clearing the garbage from the tracks? Isn't it dangerous?'

'Life is a risky business and making a living even riskier.' She smiled and pulled out a wallet from one of her bags. 'You can have this if you want. It's a used one, but not bad at all. Sometimes I find things of value here.'

There was no money in it, but I pocketed the wallet anyway.

'Why do you carry two bags?'

'One is for the kachra and the other for . . . useful things.'

'And what do you do with these things that you collect?'

'Just who do you think you are, asking so many questions? Snooping for the railway police or what?'

'Hurry up, Jaya, we have to reach Jogeshwari in an hour,' a man called out to her from farther down the tracks.

'Chalo, I'll see you around. There's my husband, and like a good wife I'll follow him to Jogeshwari now.'

I waved to her as she picked up pace.

I kept bumping into Jaya and the other workers. A railway contractor from her village in Madhya Pradesh had recruited them. She said I reminded her of her younger son—the one who had died of typhoid. Maybe that was why she was always handing me something or other.

The first time I heard it, I thought someone had their TV on at full volume, but exactly a week later, again on a Sunday morning, there was the same high-pitched singing in an unintelligible language.

'What is that?' I asked Chacha.

'It's Sunday Mass at the church.' He smiled, pointing to his left.

I followed the sound till I reached the green-tiled ground-plus-one structure that carried a small cross at its entrance. I had passed that way often and had assumed it was someone's house. Now I could see at least fifty people crammed into that tiny space, swaying to the music.

When I returned to the shop, I asked Chacha what language they were singing in.

'Telugu,' he said. 'They are from Andhra Pradesh. Some of them are known to us.'

'And do you speak Telugu?' I asked.

'I wish I did,' said Chacha, stroking his beard wistfully. 'What a fine neighbourhood we have, so rich with different cultures, all of us living together amicably!'

'That's all very well to say until something goes wrong!' said Chachi who appeared with his daily dose of medicine. 'Don't you remember what happened to Mumbai? Have you forgotten 1992 and 1993?'

'What happened?' I asked.

'Hindus one side, and Muslims, the other! What happened to our brotherhood then?'

'I was telling Gopal about the Telugu Christian community.'

'Yes, but everyone looks after their own when there's trouble.'

'Bad things do happen, but we must not lose faith in humanity. For every negative story, there are two positive stories,' said Chacha.

'Your chacha thinks everyone is a saint! But there's too much evil in the world. At least, I feel secure here as this area is dominated by our people.'

Chachi stormed back as soon as Chacha swallowed his tablets. He rolled his eyes and shook his head.

I didn't understand what they were talking about, so I kept my mouth shut.

5

I felt like a king when Chacha handed out my first month's salary with heaps of praise, though I knew the entire amount would have to be handed over to Sanjiv Maama that evening—he had reminded me before he left for work in the morning.

It made me so happy that Chacha was so pleased with my work. His previous helper had been a lazy bugger, he said, whom he had tolerated until the boy began to pilfer cash. And then he had no one for about three months until I showed up.

In our conversations, mostly Chacha talked and I listened. Sometimes he'd read out bits of news to me. He read an Urdu newspaper that I couldn't decipher. In my family, nobody had bothered to talk to me. Either they ordered me around or rebuked me for whatever went wrong even when it wasn't my mistake—and then they slapped me around. So I wasn't used to people talking to me. Chacha knew so many things. Perhaps he was right; books help us to know things.

Whenever there was a cricket match on TV, Chacha dropped his newspaper and retreated to the kitchen. And as he watched, he gave a running commentary about what each player should do and not do. Chachi teased him that he had better apply for a job as the Indian team's coach. If Kohli scored a century or Dhoni hit a six, he'd ask Bhabhi to make nimbu pani for all of us.

As I walked back home one evening, feeling rather drained, I almost collided with Aisha!

'Don't you look where you are going?' she demanded.

'Sorry,' I stammered.

'You look worn out. What happened?'

The pari had noticed my tiredness!

'Hey, Gopal, what are you thinking?' She snapped her fingers and brought me back to the dim street lights.

I told her that I was exhausted and my head was hurting.

'You'd better come with me, Gopal. Nani has an excellent balm. Best cure for headaches.' She pulled my arm. Her touch was warm and velvety.

I protested weakly, but I did want to go with her.

'I almost forgot! Nani sent me down to buy some bread. Let's go to the shop first.'

I nodded and followed her like a calf follows its mother.

While we were waiting to be served at the shop, a wet tongue licked my fingers—it was Tiger.

'Hey, Tiger, good to see you!' I bent down to ruffle his dark coat and talked to him a bit in doggy language.

'Nani has told me never to touch a dog.' She pulled me away from Tiger, but he continued to prance around my legs. 'They can't be trusted. And jungli dogs? More so! If they bite, you'll get rabies, Nadeem Maamu says.'

'Why?' I asked.

The shopkeeper laughed. 'Tiger is not rabid. He lives at the widow Martha's house. But many people tease him because he's lame.'

She didn't look convinced, so I left Tiger alone. The shopkeeper threw a pav at him, which he gobbled up hungrily.

When we reached the steps to her home, I hesitated.

'Come,' she ordered. I followed her upstairs.

Nani was short and dumpy. She was seated in a corner, on a red rug, watching TV and she glared at me with suspicion.

'Who are you?'

The pari told her my name. I folded my hands with a half-smile.

The old lady grunted. She summoned the girl to follow her to the kitchen, gesturing to me to stay by the door. I was feeling uncomfortable. I couldn't hear what they were talking about as the TV drowned their voices.

After about five minutes, Aisha returned with the balm.

'Take this and go,' she whispered. 'Nani thinks I shouldn't talk to you. I'll meet you tomorrow. Now go!' She pushed me gently towards the steps.

I didn't understand what she meant. If she wasn't supposed to talk to me, how would she meet me tomorrow?

After I washed up, I applied the balm to my forehead and the soles of my feet. I must have fallen asleep immediately.

When I awoke, I was drenched with sweat. It was still night and I had had a bad dream.

There was a river near our house in the village, where Baba used to go fishing. A very big fish had come and swallowed everyone in my family and me! Amma used to say a nightmare means bad news. Please, no. I didn't want anything bad to happen. I said all the prayers I knew.

Grumpy and tired the following morning, I worked distractedly waiting for the bad thing to happen. Would Chacha fire me?

On his return from the mosque, Chacha sat down to talk to me. He was stroking his beard, so I knew it was something important.

'Arre, Gopal. Don't feel bad, but I want to tell you something.'

I knew what was coming!

'See, Gopal, I only mean well for you.'

I nodded. The tears had already welled up in my eyes.

'Whatever you earn here will go to the village. So, what do you get? Nothing! Are you listening to me, son?'

I nodded again, my eyes boring craters into the ground.

'Why don't you take up the job of cleaning motorbikes? The ones parked across the street. Of course, it means getting up early and having to–'

'So you don't need me here any more.'

I bit my lip, trying hard not to show my despair, but those miserable drops were slipping out and he caught the tremor in my voice.

'When did I say that? Arre, buddhu! All I'm saying is you could take on an additional job. The old cleaner has moved away and so I thought . . .'

'I can continue to work here?' I had to confirm what I thought I had heard.

'Yes, of course. But will you consider this offer? You can start tomorrow.'

'Yes, yes,' I said sheepishly and went back to the anti-rust paint job I had been doing.

As Bhabhi served lunch, she told Chacha about a death in the colony. He ate his lunch hurriedly and took off.

I sat doing very little. I was tired and feeling very hot. The small table fan made no difference. The heat was also making me drowsy.

Was I dreaming? I rubbed my eyes.

Aisha was gesticulating wildly, calling me out from the shop. I stepped out warily and looked to my right and left—no sign of Nani, thank God.

'I've come to say sorry about yesterday. See, Nani gets very worried if I talk to strangers. Once she gets to know you, she'll be okay, you understand?'

I nodded.

'Did the balm help you? Are you feeling better?' she asked.

I nodded.

She asked me where I lived. I told her.

'Oh, you live along the tracks! How exciting! I always wanted to see that side of the wall. You'll take me to your house, no?'

I didn't know what to say. I nodded. It was hard to believe that Aisha had actually come to meet me. She wanted to see where I lived. I didn't really mind it, but compared to her house, mine was a hovel.

'Tell me, how old are you?'

When I said I was almost thirteen, she clapped her hands. 'See, you and I are same-same. I'm fourteen!'

Really? I had thought she was much older. She was taller, almost grown up.

'Now tell me about your family.'

When I had finished, her smile broadened.

'I knew we'd have a lot in common. My father didn't die, but he left my mother when I was a baby. Last year, my mother died, so I've come to live here. Nani really pampers me. And Nadeem Maamu is always promising me presents from Dubai.'

'Who is Nadeem Maamu?' I asked. I had only seen her scary Nani.

'Not my real Maamu. He is Nani's sister's son. He lives in Dubai and he is very rich. When he comes to visit, he brings me lots of presents. I love gifts, but I don't get any except when he comes.'

I nodded.

'I like this school very much. We learn English also. I can teach you if you'd like. It's easy,' she said.

I nodded. Everything must be easy for her because she was a pari.

I asked her about her friends who she walked to school with.

'Yasmin and Fehmeeda? They are just my walking companions—I don't really have too many friends at school. Nani says they are all jealous of me because I come first in class. But I think it is because they have all known each other from when they were little and I am still new. Besides, I'm quite a tomboy, you know, and I am not shy and quiet. My mother used to call me her son because I climb trees, dance and sing, talk to strangers.'

I nodded some more.

'It's so hot today. Let's go and eat gola!' she said, suddenly grabbing my arm.

I told her I couldn't leave the shop. She was disappointed; I was devastated.

'Idea!' she exclaimed, snapping her fingers. 'I'll get the golas and come back.'

She darted away before I could react.

I wiped the sweat off my face with my shirt. This was turning out to be the best day so far! I had been offered an extra job and Aisha wanted to be my friend.

'I forgot to ask you which flavour you like. I like kala khatta, so I brought you the same one.'

Kala khatta would be my favourite flavour from now on.

'Do you know how I managed to get away? Nani's gone because someone has died; otherwise she never leaves me home alone. Lucky, no?' she giggled and so did I.

She kept wiping the dark brown syrup off with her sleeve as it trickled down her chin. She could talk and talk. And I didn't mind listening.

Tiger came by to lick the drips of the gola that had fallen to the ground. Watching me play with him, she reached out a tentative hand to pet him. I was so proud.

'Now I'd better go,' she said finally.

I nodded and she waved and vanished.

I went back to the shop. If only I could buy her a gift . . .

How could I forget? I did have some money. At the thirteenth-day ceremony after Amma died, each guest had handed me Rs 5 or 10, and it added up to Rs 125. I could perhaps buy a dupatta and request Bhabhi to decorate it with lace and sequins.

When Chacha returned that evening, I walked away with my hands in my pockets, whistling quietly. I climbed up my favourite tree and stayed there till it was time for Sanjiv Maama's return.

6

Diagonally across our shop one sultry afternoon, a horde assembled within minutes after the words 'Salman Khan' were flung about. Was the Bollywood star here?

I joined the group, peering over shoulders and craning my neck for a glimpse of the superstar.

Actually, it was Salman Khan's bodyguard's first cousin. He was giving a detailed account of the star's fitness regime and his latest project.

Jaya and her husband were part of the throng, having finished their duty earlier than usual. They asked me to join them for a cutting chai, but I excused myself and returned to work.

The crowd continued to exchange titbits for over an hour. I couldn't imagine how they could afford to waste working hours discussing things that hardly mattered.

'Useless and good-for-nothing, that's what these people are!' snorted Chachi, who was awakened from her slumber by the hubbub. 'You'd better not get influenced by these lafanges,' she said to me. 'And most of all, keep away from those ragpickers. They are the worst.' She glared at me as she stomped back into the house.

I have to confess I was slightly scared of the ragpickers. There were three of them—they seemed about eight, ten and twelve, judging by size—whom I would see every day at the garbage heap as I walked by. Their hair was sun-bleached, their clothes were in tatters and even the air around them reeked of rotten eggs. Their eyes seemed glazed—almost as if they were smoking up strange things—and their language was filthier than their clothes.

I stayed away from them—not that they wanted to have anything to do with me—and so did most people. Only Chacha spoke to them kindly, offering water and biscuits along with our discarded packaging material.

He said, 'Mumbaikars must never forget what a great service they are doing to the city! Yes, I understand they shouldn't be doing drugs,' he added, 'but can any of us imagine what it would be like living next to a landfill?'

How or why Chacha saw something good in everyone was beyond my understanding.

Most Sundays, a few of the Telugu Christians stopped by to chat with Chacha after worship. Their wives went in to see Chachi to discuss current topics, such as the rising prices of onions or non-violent means of getting rid of cockroaches and lizards. Chachi was always worried about hair loss, and asked everyone for a suitable remedy, especially these women who had long, well-oiled plaits. The younger women showed off their gold ornaments to Bhabhi as they hummed the latest Bollywood numbers. The current favourite was 'Dagabaaz Re' from *Dabangg* 2. Their heavily accented Hindi was largely incomprehensible to me, but they always smiled at me and said friendly things I did not always understand.

The widow Martha, though, was something else! She snarled at anyone and everyone, so most people didn't get in her way. I did not like her very much, but Bhabhi said that she was one of the kindest people she knew and when anyone was in trouble, she was always there to help. Looking at her grim expression, I hoped I was never in trouble!

Tiger accompanied the widow Martha to church and back, so I got to play with him often. The pretty young girl whom I had seen Raja with in the ashram was Martha's niece Stella. She seemed very smart, and she and Bhabhi chatted a lot.

But as the days went by and the heat grew, the only thing everyone could talk about was, when would the rains come?

At last, the clouds darkened. A few harmless drops were followed by sheets of water that almost drowned the neighbourhood.

Back at home, the rain used to be largely silent; as soon as it fell, it would be swallowed up by the scorched earth. Here it clattered noisily as it fell on rooftops, tin sheets and tarpaulin, eventually running off the tarred road into rivulets in the dirt. I looked longingly at the children dancing in the street. Chachi told them to go home or they would fall sick, but no one listened.

Raja appeared on his motorbike.

'C'mon, Gopal, let's drive through this deluge.'

'Can't, I'm working.'

'You can go, beta. No one's likely to come to the shop in this weather,' Chacha intervened gently.

I ran to the motorbike despite Chachi's protests. Raja drove like a madman, but I was enthralled. It felt like we were riding through a river.

I don't know how many wet and twisty lanes he took me through before reaching the maidan. We melted into the gang of footballers. Everyone was too busy having fun to take any notice of me. Even Yakub and Imtiaz, the cricketers, offered me a half-smile. There was boisterous, rowdy dhamaal with the colony boys—like my friends and I used to do in my village.

On the way home, Raja asked if I would make him a kadak chai.

'Why not?' I said.

By the time he had finished peeing outside our shack, the tea was ready. He tried squeezing out the rainwater from his shirt and jeans, finally took them off and hung them over the door. I gave him my towel to dry himself.

'I should have had a little brother like you, always at my beck and call.' He beamed at me, thumping my back.

With a mock salute, I said, 'Bhaiyya!' and we both laughed.

'What kind of job do you do?' I asked him.

'Job? There's no money in jobs. I'm into business,' he replied.

'What kind?'

'A bit of this and a bit of that,' he said.

'Meaning what?' I persisted.

'I help people to buy and sell property.'

'Okay,' I said. 'And Stella, she's a friend of yours?'

The cup almost fell out of his hands.

'Did you see us together?'

I nodded.

He thought for a moment. 'I might as well tell you, but don't you dare share this information with anyone!'

I shook my head.

'I like her a lot. One of these days I'm going to propose to her,' he said.

'Oh nice,' I said.

'Remember, not a word to anyone,' he warned, 'otherwise I'll smash you to a pulp!'

He got up, yanked his clothes off the door, pulled them on and thundered off.

I cleaned up as best as I could before kneading the dough for aloo parathas. Sanjiv Maama grumbled about wading home through the water and having to eat my burnt, uneven parathas.

I ignored him and snuggled into my bedding, but the rain pounding on the asbestos roof of our shack was so loud that I found it difficult to fall asleep. And when I could not sleep, I started worrying. Would my second job end before it had quite begun? There would be hardly any need to wash the motorbikes in the monsoons.

The following morning, I found out that I needn't have worried. Chacha said even if it rained, I had to wipe the motorbikes clean.

The monsoon was erratic in any case. Sometimes it poured all day and all night, and then for a whole week we were rainless. Baba used to say if there's wind, the rain will be blown away; if it's hot as hell, the rain is likely to strengthen. And he was mostly right, back at home. But Mumbai rains were something else, completely unpredictable.

The roads and buildings looked like they had been swept and swabbed. The dust on trees had disappeared, revealing the true colour of the leaves. And soon, I found I had no trouble sleeping, however loud the rain on the roof of the shack.

The heat was stinging on dry days. And every possible disease attacked the colony—dengue and dysentery, malaria and diarrhoea, each more deadly than the other. The municipal dispensary was overflowing and the private doctor in the gully was making money by the bagfuls.

Luckily, Sanjiv Maama and I took turns to fall ill; one cooked and cleaned while the other tried to recover. I didn't skip work even for a day.

Chachi was so impressed with my devotion to work that she made pumpkin soup every day since I had fever. I got well at record speed because I couldn't bear the foul liquid any more.

7

News from Lakhimpur Kheri wasn't good. Floods were ravaging the state. It happened every year, but this year was even more deadly. River Sarda was greedily swallowing everything in her way. Our village was not affected that much, but the roof of the house was leaking and one of the walls had collapsed.

Sanjiv Maama was fuming because he didn't know how and where to get the money for repairs. He took to drinking every evening and cursing me for all our troubles.

That evening, Sanjiv Maama hurled the vilest abuses at me because the dal was extra spicy. He called me a spoilt little rajkumar—because Chacha fed me lunch every day, I was so stuffed that I didn't bother about the evening meal.

When he settled down by the door to smoke his bidi, he began to laugh like a jackal. I was washing the dishes outside the shack, taking care to make as little noise as possible.

'Come here,' he shrieked.

I left the dishes and stood before him.

'Ramazan begins next week. Do you know what that means?'

I thought best to say nothing.

'You should know—you are half a Muslim now, since you are with that family all the time.' He stubbed out the bidi, laughing even more loudly. 'Ab ayega mazaa! It's the month of fasting so they won't cook food all day! Now you'll know what hunger means. God will punish you for treating your maama so badly. Remember, no water also.'

His phone beeped and he stopped laughing. It was his wife. As always, she asked him to send money and he got so enraged that he flung the phone far away. He barked at me to go look for it.

I wanted to say it was too dark to find it now and I would look in the morning, but I didn't want any more trouble, so I walked along the tracks, picking up whatever looked remotely similar.

I was hoping against hope that the search wouldn't take all night. Thankfully, the phone rang, the screen lit up and I was able to retrieve it quite intact. The rascal was lucky; I had expected it to be completely damaged.

When I asked Bhabhi about Ramazan, she said it was her favourite month.

'Why?' I asked.

'It's our holiest month. I pray lots and Allah never fails to grant my wishes at the end of the month.'

Her dimples deepened.

Overhearing our conversation, Chachi added, 'She is going to pray extra hard so that Jamir gets leave to come for Eid!'

'Ammiji,' she said and they exchanged loving looks. Bhabhi saw him only once a year as he worked in Qatar; I did so want to meet Jamirbhai as I had heard stories galore about him.

On the first day of Ramazan, I drank half a litre of water and stuffed a thick roti into my mouth before showing up at the shop; I wanted to be well prepared for the day ahead.

Bhabhi appeared with our lunch at 1 p.m.

'Aren't you fasting?' I asked.

'Ammiji and I are. But Abbaji needs to eat because of his sugar problem.'

'Haan, beta, the doctor has strictly forbidden fasting.'

Bhabhi must have seen the relief on my face, for she broke into a smile.

'Gopal, you silly boy! I would have cooked for you even if we were all fasting! How could I let you go hungry?'

She and Abdul Chacha both laughed.

'And don't forget, you must have iftari before going home!'

I nodded guiltily, not sure what iftari was. But by evening, I knew exactly what it was!

Pakore, halwa and fruits arrived on a big platter like at a wedding feast. I decided I liked Ramazan, especially the way the fast was broken.

Bhabhi requested me to fetch chicken before going home. I was laughing to myself as I thought of Sanjiv Maama's gloomy prediction. Ramazan was turning out to be the best month so far!

Loping across the street, I saw the garbage truck on its evening round. By now I was friends with the garbage collectors—those on the morning shift as well as those on the evening one. Vishal was slumped over the steering wheel.

'Jai Bhim! Why are you so fagged out today?'

'Jai Bhim!' He lifted his head reluctantly. 'Stuck on the bridge for more than forty-five minutes.'

'Why, an accident or something?'

'No accident. Just waiting for some murga to pass.'

'How come? I thought you didn't mind running over chickens, dogs or even humans. All in a day's work for you types.'

'Le, phirki le, meri. I'm not talking of birds. Murga means some VIP. The cops had blocked the traffic on our side so that the guy sitting in his nice-smelling AC car could drive away smoothly.'

Aisha was at the foot of the stairs going up to her home. She said she had gone to fetch yoghurt for the pakore ki kadhi Nani was going to prepare.

'I'm totally drained!' she whispered.

'What happened? Exams?'

'No, silly! It's the first day of Ramazan and it takes a while to get used to fasting!'

'You too? Isn't fasting for grown-ups?'

'Of course not! I kept seven fasts when I was just ten years old. This year, all the girls in my class are fasting for the whole month.' She laughed and disappeared.

Later, I asked Chacha if it was necessary for children to keep a fast.

'Why not?' He chuckled. 'It's nice to learn self-control at a young age. If you can manage it, you should.'

The whole neighbourhood felt different during Ramazan. Daytime was quiet, but as soon as the sun set, the street transformed into a mela. The smells from each home were overpowering!

Aisha began to drop in at Chacha's every other evening, carrying something that Nani had made for iftari. In return, Bhabhi usually gave her something or other. At first, I refused to eat the formidable Nani's preparation but gave in when I saw the others enjoying it. Nani's khatte aloo were the best I had ever eaten! I told her when she came by next, but she just looked gloomy.

Raja dropped in with Yakub and Imtiaz for iftari, so did the widow Martha and Stella and some of the Telugu Christians.

I felt it was unfair. Bhabhi was fatigued after fasting all day and then she had to cook for guests as well. She said she enjoyed it, but if I was feeling so sorry, I could help her. That's how I began to cut up the fruit every evening; sometimes apples and bananas or papaya and guavas.

We were all counting the days to Eid, most of all Bhabhi.

One afternoon, Bhabhi took the inchtape and measured me out. Why, I asked. She only smiled.

Chacha said they were going to the wholesale market to buy material for themselves and kurta pyjama for the men. When they returned,

I accompanied Bhabhi to the ladies' tailor, a few shops down our street.

Posters of Bollywood stars in dazzling costumes were plastered on the walls. After studying the photographs in a fashion magazine, Bhabhi chose the designs that she wanted for her salwar suits. She told him to deliver the clothes on the promised date, without fail.

When we had passed Faizan Caterers on our way to the tailor's, Bhabhi joked with Faizan about sampling his biryani. He smiled and waved without taking his eyes off the pot.

That was without doubt the shop with the best smells. Painted pistachio green, it was bare, except for the wooden racks with their pots ranging in size from big to biggest. Cutlery, cheap and shineless, was stacked upon these racks besides melamine side plates, dinner plates and bowls. Gunnysacks of onions, potatoes and rice lay on the floor against the far end of the wall. The action spilled out from the room to the narrow veranda and almost on the road, where cooking and washing was taking place non-stop from 8 a.m. to 8 p.m.

Our gully had everything! There was no need for any of us to go anywhere else.

There was a sudden commotion in front of the chicken shop. It was Bismillah running after his chickens! Bhabhi told me to stop laughing and help him gather the birds.

Back home in the village, it was one of my evening chores. So I considered myself something of an expert. But it was something else in our gully! Grabbing the birds and at the same time dodging vehicles was scary and thrilling.

A couple of other boys joined the chase. Bismillah kept cursing his careless assistant for leaving the door open after the feed. 'They'll all end up in the biryani,' he muttered under his breath.

In about twenty minutes, we had gathered most of the chickens and put them back in their filthy cages. Bismillah's thanks included a ten-rupee note. I refused the money, so he thumped my back, flashing me a paan-stained smile.

When I asked Chacha what Bismillah had meant by 'they'll end up in the biryani', he told me that Bismillah and Faizan had a running disagreement. Faizan's abba, who had set up the shop twenty years ago, had bought his chickens from Bismillah's father. But now that it was Faizan who ran the show, he preferred to cycle every morning to his trusted butcher in the Malad West market for the freshly slaughtered goat meat and chicken. Bismillah resented that Faizan never bought his broilers, even at a discount. Envious competitors swore that cat meat made its way into the fragrant biryani. While Faizan wasn't unaware of these stories, he didn't care as his customers kept growing.

It seemed like someone had cast an evil eye on our celebratory mood.

Jamirbhai's leave was cancelled at the last minute, so Eid came and went silently. Chachi's and Bhabhi's smiles disappeared for a few days.

Dressed in my new kurta pyjama on Eid, I kept running into the bedroom to see what I looked like in the mirror. Bhabhi distributed sheer khurma to the neighbourhood as usual, although her heart wasn't in it; and many shared theirs with us. Sanjiv Maama dropped in, so did Raja, Tony and company. Aisha and Nani also arrived to wish Chacha, but left quickly on receiving Bhabhi's listless response. I felt I would burst, but I just couldn't have enough of the rich gooey sheer khurma.

8

Perched on my tree, swinging my legs to keep the mosquitoes at bay, I was feeling good. Six months in the city, six months at the cycle shop, five months into my second job—and responsible now for ten motorbikes! I now had savings—I gave all my bike-cleaning money to Bhabhi to keep safely.

There was much talk today about a building that had collapsed in Mazagaon—apparently many people were killed. But Mumbai was so big that Mazagaon seemed as far away as Lakhimpur, and it did not affect my mood.

The bikes I washed belonged to people who lived near Chacha. Chacha had shown me a bucket and a rag I could use from the shop. For water, he had pointed me towards the taps just outside the community toilets, which were stinky and dingy. This work wasn't easy especially because of the heat, but my earnings were growing in tandem with the number of bikes in my charge. That thought kept me going.

After washing ten bikes, I would be fully drenched and I would go home to change before heading to the cycle shop. The flip-flops that had served me well for over a year now were wearing out fast.

In these six months, I had become so familiar with the narrow bylanes leading off Squatters Colony gully that I could get anywhere. I could reach that big busy road in minutes if I snaked my way through those alleys. Some of them were dark and smelly, and you never knew what would fall on your head from the homes above, but I knew which shops were where and many of the houses.

Nowadays, Aisha would meet me almost every day, either on her way to school or on her way back or sometimes on her errands in the evenings.

Think of the pari and the pari appears! It must be part of her magic.

'Hey,' she said, peering up the tree at me. 'I'd love to get up there.'

I straightened up, wiping my hands on my shorts. I leaned as far forward as I could without falling off the tree and reached out for her hand. I was still far away!

'Here, come.'

'Not now, stupid, do you think Nani would allow me to sit up there? And with you? Never.'

'Then you'd better go. Go home to your nani.'

'Of course I will! But first let me give you the good news. I got 85 per cent in the test! The teacher liked my essay so much she read it out to everyone!'

'What was so good about your essay?'

'We had to write about what we want to become when we grow up. I wrote about becoming a pilot!'

'Pilot? Then will you take me for a spin in your aircraft? High up above the clouds.'

'Sure . . . And you, what do you want to be when you grow up?'

'Don't know.'

'Our teacher says you must plan for it. But first you have to go to school, no?'

I had never thought of becoming anything, I guess I just wanted to keep working with Chacha till I died.

She continued, 'When Nani's not around, I'll come and sit on the tree with you. Pukka.'

I knew that meant never; her nani looked out for her like a hawk.

As Aisha walked away, she shouted from across the street, 'Do you even know what this tree is called?'

'No. Never seen it in our village,' I said.

'It's called rain tree and it's not native to India. Its botanical name is *Samanea saman*. But you won't know these things because you don't go to school!'

Some passers-by looked up at me. I scowled. Why did she have to rub it in each time?

To my surprise, about a week later, she did make good on her promise. Even better, she brought a paper cone of roasted peanuts. And Tiger.

It was a beautiful evening with a gentle breeze. We played a game where she was tossing peanuts into my open mouth. Her aim was really good.

She asked me to tell her about my village.

Most of the stories I told her were true, but some had to be embellished; how else would I hear her laughter continue for a full minute or those eyes widen in fear?

I don't know why I remembered this story, since it was one of the most horrible things that had happened and I preferred to forget it. It had happened a little before Amma died. Some elders of our community decided to build a five-foot statue of Babasaheb Ambedkar near a bus stop.

'What's wrong with erecting a statue?' asked Aisha.

'Baba said the upper castes felt such a tall statue of an SC was disrespectful. Our side didn't listen, so a bloody war broke out. They came with swords, set fire to the crops; even children were butchered.'

'Didn't the police intervene?'

I snorted. 'The police look the other way when the upper castes are involved.'

'Was the statue finally built?'

'No. But Sanjiv Maama told me that the gram panchayat has given permission for building a two-foot statue in the school courtyard.'

'Thank god I'm Muslim! We don't have this caste business.'

'That's what you think! There are Dalit Muslims also,' I said.

'Really? Must be in the villages . . . I have to go home and complete my homework.'

'Do you like doing homework?' I asked.

It seemed so strange to me that she would want to study. But maybe paris were different.

'If I want to be a pilot, I have to have very good marks,' she said. 'Nadeem Maamu says that if I do, he will pay for my training.'

She smiled and threw the last peanut down at Tiger. 'You know how clever Tiger is, no? Every morning, he knows when Nani has gone to get milk and he comes to my house and begs for biscuits. Every morning without fail!'

I started another story to stop her from going away, about the mad woman who used to beg by the temple.

'If passers-by didn't part with their coins, she would let loose a string of abuses. Once, when the ration shop owner came with his new son-in-law in a shiny jeep, she blocked their entry and yelled at them. The shopworkers warned her to move away, but she stood her ground. That's when they pushed her and the poor woman fell and broke her hip bone and has been limping ever since.'

'Your village seems to be full of cruel people. Don't you agree people are much kinder to each other in Mumbai?'

I nodded.

Night after night, we were awakened by flashes of light and deep rumblings accompanied by strong showers. The plastic sheets jamming the cracks in our roof were ripped away one night, exposing our shack to the gusts of wind. Pots and pans clattered to the floor. Luckily, Chacha had a couple of spare sheets that Sanjiv Maama used to fix the roof the following evening.

When Sanjiv Maama asked how much he should pay, Chacha waved him away. He said I was his lucky charm—business had picked up after I started working for him.

I had not seen Raja for a couple of weeks. His friend Tony, who dropped by one day, told me that they were busy with arrangements for Ganesh puja.

One of the things I had heard about Mumbai long before I had come here was about Ganesh puja. Baba had come to visit Sanjiv Maama and see the celebration a couple of years ago. He had said there was singing and dancing and an endless supply of mithai for ten days. I was wondering if it would be even bigger than Eid.

Tony asked Chacha for a donation for the festival. Chacha gave him a fifty-rupee note and sent him off with his good wishes.

'That's the beauty of living in this country—we all share in each other's celebrations,' said Chacha, patting his beard.

'I don't know if it's beauty or duty,' said Chachi. 'It's like a tax we pay for peaceful coexistence.' She was sweeping the front room, gathering the strands of hair that were strewn over the floor. She always complained that she must be surely shedding more hair than Tiger.

'You are way too cynical, Ammiji,' Chacha said with a frown.

'And you, too trusting,' said Chachi with a matching frown.

I asked if we would all visit the neighbourhood Ganesh mandal together.

'You can go with your chacha,' said Chachi, vanishing into the house.

He nodded vigorously.

9

When Bhabhi and I had finished our tuition class one evening, I whined to her to make good on her promise of the visit to the seaside.

'When, Bhabhi, when will we go to the beach? Marve Beach or Juhu Beach, any one will do!'

'Yes, of course! Sorry, Gopal. What with one thing and another, I forgot about it . . . Why don't you go with Raja?'

'No, I want to go with you.'

'Fine. We'll plan an outing one evening after the rains are over.'

'Yay! But . . . will Chacha object if I leave the shop?' My hopes suddenly crashed.

'You know Abbaji. He will certainly not mind if we go one evening. Once these tests are done, I'll be freer,' she said with her quiet smile.

Her words sent my heart soaring to the twenty-second floor of the blue-white building.

There was one particular reason why I wanted to go with Bhabhi. Maybe, just maybe, Bhabhi wouldn't mind if Aisha came along too. That would be beyond compare—going to the beach with my favourite people . . .

I was whistling with extra vigour while chopping the onions and kneading the dough as I imagined being on the beach . . .

Suddenly, Sanjiv Maama strode in and knocked me to the ground with one almighty slap. And then he kicked me ferociously on my knee.

'You cheat! Hiding things from me? You think I wouldn't get to know!'

He yelled some more and threw a few more kicks at me. I curled up on the floor into as tight a ball as I could and covered my face with my arms.

'What is wrong?' I panted.

'Playing innocent, huh? Shaitan ki aulad! I should never have brought you along. You'll be parcelled off by tomorrow's train.'

The thought of going back chilled me. I stayed curled up, trying not to moan.

'Sneaking behind my back to take a second job and not giving me a paisa of that salary! Ten bikes! I feed you, but you pocket the money. My own flesh and blood betraying me.'

The blows rained down, and soon, blessedly, I knew no more.

Even before I opened my eyes, I was aware of intense pain. Every part of my body was hurting badly. I couldn't move my limbs.

I shuddered as the memory of my maama came flooding back. I hoped he was not around. I could not take more beatings.

'He's up, Abbaji!' The voice was sweet–Bhabhi?

I opened my eyes a little. I was in Chacha's house–in the inside room. How had I come here?

I tried sitting up but could not. Bhabhi came and put a cool hand on my forehead.

Chacha burst in. 'Praise be to Allah, you are conscious! For days, we've been praying for the temperature to go down.'

I tried to speak but before I could, Chacha shushed me. 'The widow Martha had said that you need absolute quiet, beta. And rest.'

Wondering what the widow Martha had to do with me, I drifted back to sleep.

Much later, when I had woken and eaten and had medicines, Bhabhi told me the whole story. When I had not turned up for work, Chacha had called Sanjiv Maama who had not answered several calls. Chacha had then come to the shack because he thought both of us were ill.

Instead, he found me alone and badly bruised. He had called a rickshaw and bundled me into it.

They hadn't gone to the municipal health centre because then the police would have got involved. Instead, they had called the widow Martha because she used to be a nurse. She had tended to my bruises and given me a shot to relieve the pain. Then had followed a few days of fever, when I had floated in and out of consciousness. The widow Martha, Chachi and Bhabhi had stayed up nights to take care of me.

Bhabhi mimicked how Sanjiv Maama had slunk away with hands folded after Chacha's dressing-down.

'He wants to send me back to the village!' I said in panic, remembering our last conversation.

'Don't worry,' Bhabhi said calmly. 'Abbaji won't let that happen. He has threatened your uncle with a police report if he so much as raises his voice or lays a measly finger on you ever again.'

I was so relieved that within a few hours, I was up on my feet. Lying in bed was getting boring.

When I looked into the mirror, I wished I hadn't. There were blue, black and purple bruises all over. My lower lip was cut and swollen. There was a big gash above my left eye. No wonder the pain was excruciating. Chacha assured me that it would all heal in some days.

Yadav, the guava seller, popped in to see me for a while. He and I had become good friends as he parked his cart near the cycle shop in the late mornings. On slow mornings, we'd chat and he'd offer me a guava for free.

I crawled back into bed in a couple of hours and fell asleep only to wake the next morning. The pain persisted, but I felt stronger. Bhabhi brought me a glass of milk and roti.

Chachi made trotters soup for lunch; I hated the oily brew, but she stood there till I had gulped it down. 'It's good for your bones,' she said sternly.

'What about the Ganesh festival?' I asked.

'It's in full swing, but you are in no state to step out of the house,' said Chacha gently. 'Don't worry—the festival will be back next year. Right now let's concentrate on building your strength.'

Aisha appeared in mid-afternoon, when the heat was at its peak. The sweat was pouring out of every pore in my body, making me squirm.

'Are you still in pain? I prayed so hard for you, you know.' She did not wait for me to answer, but carried on with her own news. 'Did Bhabhi tell you the good news? My Nadeem Maamu is going to pay us a visit. Coming after two whole years! He asked me what I wanted and I gave him a long list of things. Nani scolded me, but I can't help it if he asked me?'

I nodded.

'He's bringing me a mobile! Isn't that awesome? I can call all my friends. But you, you don't have a phone. How will I talk to you?'

'You meet him every day, child, you don't need a phone to talk to him,' said Chacha.

'Yes, of course, I forgot!' said she, laughing.

I was feeling tired at all this excitement, and when I saw Nani walking in, I got up to go in. She did not ask me how I was but told Aisha sternly to go home at once and study for her tests.

I was near the door when I heard Nani tell Chacha, 'Sorry, Abdul bhai, she's a girl after all. I don't like her talking to boys, especially this one.'

I stopped behind the curtain to listen.

'Gopal?' said Chacha, sounding surprised.

'That low-caste boy who works for you.'

'That's Gopal. He's a good boy, Aapa!' said Chacha.

I peeked through the gap between the curtain and the wall.

'You don't know what it is to have a teenaged girl at home. No mother, no father, I only see to everything. It is a big burden for me.' She sighed deeply.

'Does Aisha's father send you any money for her upbringing?'

'Not one paisa! He hasn't looked back since he walked out on my daughter! I have my savings and Nadeem is very helpful. That boy dotes on Aisha, always telling all our relatives how bright she is, mashallah! And now that he's coming, he's going to bring her lots of presents, he says. Aisha is so excited.'

'Yes, Aisha mentioned that he's coming.'

'Probably in May. What will happen when he gets married . . . His wife may control the purse strings, who knows?'

'You worry too much, Aapa. Allah takes care of everything.'

'Ah, that's so easy for you to say; nobody understands my tension. That's why I suffer from high blood pressure. I'd better get back, Aisha's alone. Khuda hafiz, Abdul bhai!'

I remained inside. I was livid about what Nani thought of me but at the same time saddened for what she had said about Aisha. It was only

September—her maamu's visit was still a long way away, and she was already so excited.

Raja arrived to inquire about my health. He was jubilant as he had returned from a darshan of Mumbai's biggest Ganesh mandal, Lalbaugcha Raja. Because of his contacts, he had had to queue for only six hours. He stuffed the prasad into my mouth, saying it had the power to speed up my recovery.

He even offered to bash up my uncle; Chacha shut him up by saying that was no way to settle conflicts.

When Chacha had stepped inside for something, Raja produced a red plastic box from the pocket of his jeans. 'Hey Gopal, got to show you something!'

He snapped it open under my nose. It contained a sparkling ring.

'What do you think? It's for Stella. It's been blessed by Lalbaugcha Raja!'

'Nice.'

'Just nice? This damn thing's set me back by Rs 15,000, saala. But I'm sure she'll like it. It's made of gold and that stone may not be real diamond, but who cares? It's called American diamond. See how it glitters?'

I nodded. It was very sparkly.

'And see this? Got to keep the widow Martha happy as well.' He chuckled.

It was a leather collar for Tiger, studded with a large cross made of brass.

'I'm sure Tiger will be very happy. His old one is a bit frayed,' I said, examining the collar.

'The dog matters more to you than my Stella? Can't blame you, you are too young to understand the pull of the loins. It's been a long day; I'd better get going!'

He rode away, waving at me, delirious with joy.

A part of me didn't want my strength to come back—it meant going back to our shack! But how long could I remain here?

Rather reluctantly, I declared after about a week that I should go home. Bhabhi protested the most, but Chacha convinced her that I was free to go if I wanted to.

My steps slowed down as I approached the shack. Climbing over the ladder was painful. I was as afraid as a man might be, facing a hungry hyena. Chacha was positive that Sanjiv Maama wouldn't dare beat me up again, but I was not so sure.

I decided my safest option was to pretend to be asleep before he returned so that there would be no need for conversation. Sanjiv Maama came, ate his food and went to sleep in his corner of the shack, without saying a word to me.

For the next week or so, Chacha forbade me from doing any real work, so I sat around most of the day. Business was slow anyway as it was exam season.

The only entertainment came from the tuition children, who came for twice as long. Sameera and Rizwan were always taking my help to solve the tests that Bhabhi created for them, in spite of Bhabhi's scoldings.

Chacha would read to me from the newspaper. Every other day, there were riots in some part of the country, sometimes Hindu-Muslim, sometimes Hindu-Christian, sometimes upper castes with SCs. This time he was reading about the Muzaffarnagar riots in my home state.

'These clashes have been described as the worst violence in Uttar Pradesh in recent history! Sixty dead, ninety-three injured and over 50,000 displaced! So shameful!' said Chacha.

'Why do people keep having the same fights over different gods?' I asked Chacha.

'God isn't responsible for our divisions. It's we humans who differentiate and segregate,' said Chacha.

I couldn't figure out what he was saying. This god and religion business seemed too messed up. Maybe we should do away with religion altogether.

From time to time, Chacha asked me about Sanjiv Maama's behaviour. I had nothing to report; let alone talk, we didn't even make eye contact. But I despised him with all my heart and longed for the day I could get away from him.

But when I shared my hatred for Sanjiv Maama with Chacha, I received a lecture on compassion and mercy and stuff. While I listened to Chacha for most things, I couldn't forgive Sanjiv Maama. No way. Better to keep my thoughts hidden; why invite another sermon?

10

I ran into Jaya at the chai stall. I had not seen her for a while.

And Tiger came trotting by wearing his brand-new collar. Seeing the way he slobbered over me and my equally enthusiastic response, Jaya promised to bring something for the dog next time.

'Do you ever find things for girls, you know, like a handbag or anything pretty that girls would like?'

'Wah, beta, you've got a girlfriend? At such a young age, huh?' She laughed gruffly, pinching my arm hard.

'No, no, nothing like that!' I started to walk away. Tiger followed me.

'Arre, Gopal, I won't ask you why you want it! Next time I find a trinket, I'll save it for you.'

Singing about love being in the air, she paid the chaiwallah and crossed the street to return to work.

I wanted to say that she could keep the trinkets to herself, but Aisha was bounding towards me, as she took something out from her school bag.

'You won't believe what we are going to do tomorrow!'

It was a pair of bright yellow rubber gloves. She started pulling them on.

'We?'

'My classmates and I. We are going to clear the rubbish from this street!'

'This street? It's so dirty!'

'That's why we need to clean it!'

'Why? Are the municipal workers on strike?'

'No, our teacher said we must take responsibility for our surroundings. No class tomorrow, only cleaning!'

She went past me, waving her arms in the air, and then stopped and turned to me. 'You'll come, no? You can also help us. My teacher will give you a pair of gloves.'

'I can't leave the shop. And to tell you the truth, I'm not interested.'

'Not interested?!'

She looked a bit annoyed as she went off. I turned back to resume my duties.

As the afternoon changed to evening, I kept imagining Aisha sweeping the street. How black and dusty her face would be! Ugly blisters forming on her hands. She had no idea what she was getting into. The school should stick to teaching, why did it expect kids to clean the roads? It must definitely be a form of punishment for some mischief.

Chacha got annoyed because my pace of work was so slow.

Finally, I thought of something! I left work a little early so that I wouldn't miss the garbage truck on its evening round.

I waited by the disgusting heap, swatting flies and dodging rats. When the truck showed up, I waved to Vishal. As soon as the two guys hopped off its stinky rear, I popped up with a 'Jai Bhim'.

'Hey Gopal, what's up? Slacking off today?' asked Jadhav.

'No, no. I came to tell you something important. Tomorrow the schoolkids are coming here. They are supposed to clean the area.'

'Wah, we needn't come tomorrow then!' Jadhav slapped Kamble on his back. Kamble, occupied in hauling up the rubbish, didn't bother to listen to Jadhav's words.

'No, please listen to me. Can you really clean it up today? I mean really polish off every last bit?'

'Are you going to be chatting to Gopal all evening or what?'

Once Vishal yelled at them, that was it. The green devil zoomed off, leaving most of the garbage exactly where it was before the truck arrived.

Aisha called out to Chacha as she and her brigade marched by. They were accompanied by the skirt-and-blouse-clad girls from the neighbouring English school. She was soon lost among the other girls; in spite of craning my neck, I couldn't spot her.

Chacha stepped out to talk to the teachers and called out to Bhabhi to serve them water.

Once the girls had gone, Chacha stroked his beard and praised the schools for instilling good habits in the children. I looked at him disbelievingly.

The street did look marginally cleaner in the evening, but the garbage heap looked the same, if not worse. Their efforts hadn't made an iota of difference.

That evening, I hung around on the pavement opposite her house, waiting for Aisha to come out to the balcony. I just wanted to know if she was all right. Instead, Nani appeared on the balcony and shot me a look filled with loathing.

As I glared at the ground beneath my feet, a motorbike screeched to a halt by me.

It was Raja, of course. He thumped me hard on the back and almost yanked me off the ground with his one-armed hug. 'Come, sit. Let me take you for a ride! How about a kulfi?'

I said I had to return home to cook dinner.

'Won't you ask why I'm so happy?'

'Why?' I asked, without a shred of interest.

'Stella absolutely adored the ring! We are as good as engaged, but she's not yet sure if the widow Martha approves of me, so we are waiting for the right moment. Meanwhile, I'm going to organize the cataract surgery for the widow. That will raise me up a notch or two in her eyes,' he added, grinning widely. 'And that Stella will give up her silly job ideas . . .'

With a triumphant wave, he revved up and thundered away.

Unfortunately, Sanjiv Maama had started talking to me bit by bit. It was mostly instructions—do this, do that. But when he got news from home, it made him chatty.

A Dalit woman had become the new sarpanch, which had made all the upper castes mad.

Both sides had raised flags and shouted slogans in the chowk. Then there had been stone pelting and the sarpanch had received a deep gash and many others had been injured. The next day, there had been a morcha in support of the new sarpanch. My aunt had been part of it, and then the upper-caste people had attacked them and someone had smeared cow dung on my aunt's face.

I was very impressed that our people were fighting; Baba and Amma always said it was our fate. But Sanjiv Maama was, of course, mad at his wife.

'What business did she have of getting involved in this quarrel? She should work in the fields and mind the children. Leave the rest to menfolk to sort everything out!' he yelled at me.

I just nodded.

Sanjiv Maama's friend's moustache was shaved off because he dared to go to the cinema hall in Lakhimpur. I thought this was funny, but Sanjiv Maama was still mad. 'We are as human as anyone else!' he thundered. 'How long can they treat us like dirt?'

I was so deeply engrossed in counting the day's earnings at Chacha's shop that I almost missed the fakir's cry. Chacha was away and I only noticed when Chachi rushed out to await his arrival.

The fuzzy-haired fakir was on his regular round of the colony, shouting some mumbo jumbo, interspersed with the word 'Allah'. The stray dogs, which lazed around all day, made it their business to chase him and he pelted them with stones and choice words. Tiger also joined the chase but abandoned it midway because his slow trot made him an easy target.

The fakir's cry got louder as he neared our shop and Chachi rushed out to the street to invite him in. She talked with him in low tones for about ten minutes in one corner of the shop. Then I could hear her call out to Bhabhi to come down immediately.

I was curious by this time and tried to listen to what was being said.

When Bhabhi appeared, the fakir pulled out a feather duster from his smelly bag, patted her head with it, fished out a talisman from his pocket and tied it to her upper right arm, all the time muttering some chants. With her head bowed, Chachi presented him two hundred-rupee notes.

The dignity of his exit was a bit ruined by Chacha's return. Chacha's scowl made the fakir take off as if his lungi was on fire.

'How dare you take this scoundrel in? Haven't I warned you to stay away from these charlatans?'

Never before had I seen Chacha spewing fire.

Chachi was in full retreat. 'It's nothing,' she muttered. 'Just a little blessing for Sana. It's high time she became a mother.' She wrapped her arm around Bhabhi, who stood still.

'Nothing, you say? Thanks to suckers like you, these guys thrive. What did you buy from him?'

Bhabhi held out her trembling arm with the talisman.

'And you, Sana. You should have more sense. What use is your degree, your education, if you fall for these superstitions?'

By now he was coughing and sputtering. Bhabhi went into the kitchen and brought him a glass of water. The talisman was no longer on her arm.

'No need to get so worked up! Not good for your diabetes,' said Chachi, before retreating to the safety of the kitchen.

Nobody talked much that whole day. I agreed with Chacha—I had heard stories of fraudsters in the surrounding villages, including the temple priests. Always making money with clever words. I wished I could do something to comfort Chachi and Bhabhi.

It took a couple of days for Chacha's anger to subside and the atmosphere in the shop to turn buoyant once again.

'How do you like this cycle?' asked Bhabhi as I was getting ready to leave the shop one evening. Tony, who had come to collect his bicycle that we had fixed, was hanging around listening to our conversation.

She was pointing to the second-hand Hero Rapid that was on sale. Chacha didn't usually buy and sell used bicycles, but he hadn't been able to turn down a distant relative's request. This one was about five years old; other than needing a new seat and new tyres, it was in tip-top condition.

'It rides very well,' I said. 'I tried it out yesterday.'

'I knew it! That's why you should have it,' smiled Bhabhi.

'Yes,' said Chacha. 'Sana is right as always! It's yours from today!'

'Mine? But . . . it's too expensive and I–'

'The money has been taken care of,' said Bhabhi, smiling mysteriously.

'I can't let you pay for it, Bhabhi!'

'Arre buddhu, it's from your own hard-earned money! Abbaji and I discussed it–you could use some of the motorbike-cleaning money towards this purchase. After all the work you do, you must spend something on yourself for Diwali and . . . it's also when your birthday is, isn't it?'

She had remembered my birthday! Nobody in my family had any record of when exactly I was born, but they remembered it was around Diwali in a year when the crops had failed.

Tony gave me a thumbs up as he left the shop.

'I can't take it home though! It would be stolen the very first day.'

'It can stay here. Anyway, you spend most of your waking hours here, don't you?' said Chacha. 'Please let Sanjiv know about it; we don't want a repeat of what happened last time.'

I couldn't believe my ears! It would be the first thing ever that I had owned. I walked towards home with a wide grin.

Back home the only excitement about Diwali every year were the rock-hard laddoos that my aunt made and the zamindar's son's discarded clothes that came my way. Thinking how jealous my bike would make Sanjiv Maama gave me an extra thrill.

As I neared the ladder to my home, Tony and his cronies accosted me.

'What will you do with so much money?' asked Tony, tapping my head.

'Not fair that you've got all this wealth stashed up! Come, let's play cards so you can lose some of it and become lighter!' said Shankar.

His friends whinnied, praising his wit.

'Wait, wait, guys! First we've got to determine what gender he belongs to! Getting beaten up by an uncle and taking cover behind Sana's dupatta, that's not the mark of a man. Real men smoke, swear and you know . . .' added Tony, trying to pull down my shorts.

I dodged his attempt, walking faster.

'How about an intro to Aisha?' said Ganpat, sending the others galloping across the street with devilish shrieks.

I wanted to pluck out his eyes for this remark, but I knew I was no match for these goons. Six of them with their rippling muscles. Worse, I could feel tears of rage come to my eyes.

I carried on walking, pushing away their hands as they manhandled me. Shankar stuck his hands into my pockets looking for money but came up with zilch.

Tony's grip on my neck tightened as they steered me to the video parlour across the flyover. There they put on a film showing naked men and women doing things to each other. I was too embarrassed to watch, but I knew I had to pretend interest, otherwise it would be worse. Then I got up to leave and each time, Tony pulled me down, more aggressively.

Finally, he got bored and told me I could go if I did some social work. There were some leaflets that he had to distribute and if I would do it for him, I could go home. I agreed instantly.

Since I had to deliver the leaflets, I was a little late for work. Chacha asked me if everything was okay.

Rather proud that I had done social work, I told him about the distribution and showed him a copy of the flyer. He read it intently and then asked me if I knew what it said. I didn't because it was written in Marathi.

'This piece of paper is inviting people to a rally about migrants coming to Mumbai and taking away jobs from the locals. It's meant to turn people in Squatters Colony against each other. I'm ashamed that you volunteered to distribute these,' he said sternly.

I felt smaller and stupider with every word he spoke. Chacha had never spoken to me like this. 'I didn't know what it was about. I just did what they told me to,' I said weakly.

'Gopal, learn to use that head of yours. Don't tell me you will jump into the well if someone asks you to.'

I shook my head. I dared not tell him what had happened; still less could I tell him how I felt since I did not know how to put it into words. I belonged nowhere. Boys like Yakub and Imtiaz ignored me—to them, I was an out-of-school labourer. The ragpickers at the garbage dump ignored me—to them, I was just another shopworker. Besides Chacha's family and Aisha, I had nobody.

Telling Chacha that I had a headache, I left earlier than usual. I took refuge in my tree and stayed up there until the mosquitoes started bothering me.

11

As soon as we got the new tyres and seat fixed, I was flying through the streets on my new acquisition.

Sameera regularly asked me to take her for a ride after tuition. She would clutch me tightly from behind, squealing with both fear and joy, and plead with me for yet another round. After examining my cycle carefully, Aisha said she wished she could cycle, but Nani would never allow her to learn. Everyone, including Yakub and Imtiaz, looked at me enviously. I was enjoying the attention, loving every bit of it!

Sanjiv Maama grumbled about my wasteful ways, saying I was so much under the influence of Chacha and family that nothing else mattered. Thankfully, he was leaving for the village two days before Diwali. On Chacha's urging, I parted with Rs 200 to buy mithai for his children.

Returning from the mithai shop with plump golden boondi laddoos, I was heading to the firecracker stall when I spotted Aisha at the dairy. I asked her to accompany me so that she could help me select the best crackers. My heart was set on the phuljhadis, chakris and anars. I had no interest in the ear-splitting bombs.

'Don't you know that we are not supposed to burst crackers?' she asked sternly.

'Why? Everybody does. And it will be my first time; I've only watched others do it,' I said.

'So what? There are sooo many reasons why we shouldn't!' she continued in a teacherly voice. 'Did you know that thousands of children—even six-year-olds—are made to work in the fireworks factories? They get burnt or develop asthma or worse still, they die! And the air and noise pollution caused by crackers is unimaginable!' She sniffed. 'Even your favourite Tiger will hate them.'

'I didn't know that,' I said.

'How will you? You don't go to school, do you?'

And that was that, of course. We went our separate ways without saying another word.

Bhabhi made crisp triangled aloo ke parathe, dripping with ghee and chawal ki kheer for Diwali. Chacha invited Yadav, the guava seller, to join us for lunch. Yadav was so grateful that he brought us more than enough guavas for a month.

I wore the pair of blue jeans and red T-shirt that Chacha and his family had presented me—'Diwali and birthday present,' smiled Bhabhi. My flip-flops were replaced by the floaters that Jaya had got me from her treasure trove.

Raja was missing; his family had gone to the village. Sameera and Rizwan brought me a 'Happy Diwali' card. Aisha was still sulking, so she didn't come over. Too bad, we finished off the laddoos that I had meant to give her.

The cold season barely touched Mumbai; the only difference being that we didn't perspire as much as before. At home, in winter we used to huddle around the fire every night before going to sleep; me and my cousins fighting over the razai and then I'd get up wide awake, in the middle of the night, more frozen than an ice gola. Gorging on roasted peanuts, red and swollen ones, was my best memory from winters at home. But still people here were wearing sweaters and all the infants were swaddled in colourful cardigans.

The ashram was unusually crowded in the evening. I stepped out without eating when a hand gripped my collar. It was Raja, beaming at me!

'Have you had prasad?' he asked me.

'No, it's okay.'

'No, it's not!! You have to eat something today! We've just concluded a shuddhikaran ceremony.' He stuffed a peda into my mouth and handed me a bowl of shrikhand. His eyes were gleaming.

'What ceremony is that?' I asked.

'You are a complete idiot, living here yet knowing nothing.' He slammed my head against the pillar affectionately. 'This ashram is famous for its purification ceremonies. Those who have lost their way and become Muslims, Christians, whatever, they can become Hindu once again here.' He pulled me closer and whispered, 'Stella will also have to go through this ceremony, you know.'

I nodded. I did not understand exactly what he was telling me, but I was intent on polishing off the sticky sweet.

A familiar voice called out to me just as I reached the ladder to my home. 'Where are you coming from?'

I looked up at her balcony. I could only make out her silhouette against the light coming from inside.

'The ashram.'

'What were you doing there? Singing bhajans?' That lovely tinkling laugh followed.

'No, I go there sometimes to eat dinner. It's free. Today we had shrikhand.'

'I don't like shrikhand. But I want to see the place. You'll take me?'

'No, you'd better not go there!'

The words flew out of my mouth before I realized I shouldn't have put it that way.

'Why not?'

I felt her eyes boring into me even though I could hardly see the outline of her face. 'Now it's late. I'll explain to you some other time.'

I disappeared before she could quiz me further.

That night my nightmares kept me alert and watchful. Whenever I tried to fall asleep, I could see the pujari chasing Aisha with a tumbler full of Ganga jal or shrikhand or whatever they used.

Someone shouted 'accident' and the whole street ground to a halt.

I didn't look up but continued pumping air into the tyre of the cycle I was working on. Train accidents were quite common and there was one every few weeks. I stayed far from these sights; blood always made me shit-scared.

At first, it was somehow compelling to see a bloodied white sheet on a stretcher, but I soon got used to it. The guys from the neighbouring shops seemed to have not—they would leave their work to go and stare at the unfortunate victim. Then they would loiter around the chai stall, describing the blood and gore. Bets were taken on whether it was a suicide or not, and if the suicide was caused by a love affair gone wrong or money trouble.

But today was different as I soon found out. It wasn't someone unknown, it was Jaya. I realized this when her husband walked past the shop, sobbing uncontrollably, by one of the two shrouded stretchers.

I left the tyre midway, I got on to my bicycle and rode in circles before hitting the highway, my tears flowing freely! My feet pedalling furiously, in the floaters she had given me, and my mind was blank. I would have perhaps continued for miles, except that a water tanker came so close it brushed my arm, waking me up from my stupor.

Sufficiently sobered, I took the service road back to the shop. Jaya, my friend, gone! She had been looking forward so much to going home for a break . . . Her raspy, jolly voice would ring in my ears for the rest of my life.

The next day, I heard from the others by the tracks that the labourers had been warned about an express train flying towards them. Jaya and her companion had panicked, lost their footing and fallen in its path, while the others scampered to safety.

Chacha showed me the small paragraph in his newspaper. I was shocked that it was just a few lines.

Chacha said, 'Their death doesn't interest people; to the newspaper people, they were just contract workers, used to walking along the tracks, who should have been more careful. People want to read about cricketers and film stars.'

'And business tycoons,' added Chachi. 'Ordinary people's lives are cheap.'

'At least her husband will receive a lakh as compensation,' said Chacha.

'With that kind of money, he'll soon find another wife!' said Chachi.

Furious with Chachi, I said, 'But he really cared for Jaya; I'm certain that he's going to free their mortgaged land with this amount!'

'That's if and when he receives the compensation,' said Chacha, scratching his beard ruefully.

'That's why I tell you time and again never to cross the tracks,' he said sternly to both Chachi and Bhabhi, who had returned from the market.

'And do you think climbing those bridges is less dangerous?' snorted Chachi before storming into the inside room.

Chacha turned his attention to me, saying, 'I hope you don't cross the tracks, Gopal.'

I shook my head. But actually I had, twice.

The first time was to impress Aisha. She had popped in unannounced one day when I was cleaning the shack. Intrigued by the intertwining tracks, she had challenged me to walk across to the western end and back. I had agreed. I didn't tell her that I accepted her dare only because it was a Sunday and the frequency of trains was low. Almost peeing in my pants, I had walked across swiftly and had returned even faster!

'You are a superhero,' she had said. She had wanted to try the same feat, but I had convinced her that Nani wouldn't approve of it. Hearing the N-word, she had vanished instantly.

The second time was because I had to. Sanjiv Maama's brother-in-law had come to Mumbai scouting for a job. He had got off in Goregaon West and couldn't figure out how to reach our place. Sanjiv Maama and I had to get across and lug his heavy suitcase home. His idiotic brother-in-law kept jabbering all the while, making our job far more difficult. Twice we had to wait while the trains whizzed past. That time I did wet my shorts, causing Sanjiv Maama much amusement.

'You would have been better off if you were born a girl,' he said with a smirk.

I was riding to the park, enjoying the cool breeze, when Raja's distinctive whistle drew my attention.

He was outside the widow Martha's house, helping with the lights and other decorations for Christmas. I stopped. Tiger was running up and down excitedly, barking at every streamer that was being put up. The widow Martha and Stella were busy in the kitchen from where some tantalizing smells wafted out.

Raja was very cheerful about how things were progressing with Stella and assured me that they would be married early the following year. It would be a good year, he said. Mumbai was growing—the monorail and the metro would be starting soon, he said—and there were lots of opportunities for a man like him. He asked me to stay on and taste the goodies being made, but I didn't want to miss my outing, so I rode away.

On Christmas Day, Chachi and Bhabhi visited the widow Martha and brought back six slices of cake. The cake was unlike anything I had eaten before. It was dark and moist, filled with raisins and god knows what else; I pulled those out and ate the rest.

Raja dropped in the next day to inform me that he had accompanied them to church and the widow Martha was beginning to warm to him. His gang was going to party at Marve Beach for New Year's Eve; he kept saying how awesome it would be with dancing and daaru and pork vindaloo and that I should go with him.

I declined his invitation. Alcohol didn't interest me and I didn't know what pork vindaloo was. Raja was tolerable, but nothing on earth could persuade me to spend the evening with those louts.

12

I had been in Mumbai more than a year, I realized one day.

The final exams were over and Bhabhi and I were at last free of our tuitions. While I wouldn't admit it to Chacha, I was beginning to enjoy this study thing. History, geography, science were all going boom boom in my head. Some nights, I walked the earth discovering ancient civilizations; other nights, I roamed the galaxies, setting up new civilizations.

In our village school, Masterji had hardly ever turned up. When he did, sometimes in a drunken state, he'd beat the hell out of us for the slightest mischief. At other times, he'd herd us all together and ask us to recite our tables or read the same lesson over and over again. If not for the daily khichdi, no one would want to see the inside of our dilapidated school building.

Bhabhi decided to squeeze in at least an hour of studies for me during the vacation. She was pushing me to enrol in the local school. I could work here the rest of the day, Chacha said. He had already approached the Hindi-medium school in our neighbourhood and they seemed willing to admit me.

Since all the kids were on holiday and the weather was not that hot, they all wanted their neglected bikes fixed. Our hands and backs ached with the vacationing children's demands.

Bhabhi and Chachi were equally busy with their annual pickle-making. I found any and every excuse to sneak into the kitchen for even half a slice of raw mango. Mmm, its sour tingle transported me to the fruit-heavy trees in our village. No tree was safe from me and my catapult back home, but here I wouldn't do anything so frivolous.

I knew that troubles come in threes, so I wondered what else would go wrong when Chacha's family was struck by two tragedies in swift succession. His daughter, Nazma, who had been expecting her first child, miscarried. Chachi was convinced that Nazma's mother-in-law must have overworked her in their rice fields. Then, to make things worse, Jamirbhai's leave was cancelled for the second time! Bhabhi was distraught and couldn't be cheered by any of my antics. Sprawled out on her bed, she kept flipping through her wedding album.

Chacha was lost for words and kept to himself. Chachi was the first to shake herself out of the collective stupor; she got Bhabhi involved in a massive clean-up operation of the cupboards in the front room.

That's how Bhabhi came upon a black chiffon dupatta that she didn't really need, so she offered to do some work on it for Aisha. Unable to hide my grin, I suggested that she use silver sequins with some matching lace.

'Anything for you,' Bhabhi said, bringing out her paraphernalia and getting down to work. Her dimples were back in place.

As school was closed, Aisha had no reason to come by. But she convinced her nani that she needed embroidery lessons from Chachi. She would come dancing in every alternate afternoon, with very little intention of using needle and thread. After a few stitches, she would be out in the shop helping me and Chacha, besides keeping up her relentless chatter.

Chacha was entertained by her bindaas ways. Most of the time it was 'Nadeem Maamu this' and 'Nadeem Maamu that' as his arrival was only days away.

The day Aisha's results were declared, she bounced in waving her report card in the air. She had stood first in the class, surpassing her own previous marks. The teachers were very proud of her. Even her curmudgeon Nani beamed as she passed around a box of pedas. She didn't even take offence when Chacha slid the box towards me.

By early May, the heat was becoming more and more unbearable. While it was tolerable at dawn, by noon it tightened its grip on you and wouldn't let go till it dropped you gasping for mercy late in the evenings.

Aisha hadn't appeared for a whole week. Trying to keep the anxiety out of my voice, I asked Bhabhi if she had heard from or met Aisha. Bhabhi told me not to worry; she would undoubtedly come to show off her uncle.

Aisha appeared the next morning with her maamu. Covered with grease, I glared at the wheel I was working on. There was nothing special about the man; of medium height and weight, he looked just like anyone else. He had on a pair of sunglasses but so did others in our colony.

When he spoke to Chacha, he cursed the filth in Mumbai and bragged about Dubai's cleanliness. Even bent over the wheel, I could see that his eyes kept roaming over Aisha, though he didn't speak to her. He said that he had big dreams for Aisha. She would be a doctor. Aisha stood next to him, demurely and quietly—unlike her usual self.

Chacha's offer of tea was declined, so I was sent to get him a Coke. When I got back, he snatched the bottle out of my hand without a word of thanks and downed the liquid in a few gulps. He fished out a gutkha sachet, stuffed his mouth with it and threw the wrapper on the shop floor. Nodding at Chacha, they sauntered off to meet other acquaintances in the colony.

That evening, I lay curled up on the rain tree far longer than usual. Waiting for the day her maamu would be gone and we could go back to being ourselves . . .

Aisha bounded in the following day and thrust her new phone in my face. In one breath, she explained all its features, showing me the pictures she had clicked and the music she had downloaded.

I tried to match her enthusiasm, but it was really not that exciting. It was a more advanced model of the one Bhabhi had, which she used to lend me to play games on slow days, so I was familiar with its working.

'Tonight we're having Faizan's biryani. I came to place the order,' she said.

'Great,' I said, handing the phone back to her.

Bhabhi came out at this inopportune moment with a plastic bag. She said, 'Aren't you forgetting Aisha's gift?'

'Gift?' Aisha's eyes sparkled as she seized the bag before I could do anything.

'It's nothing,' I said. 'Bhabhi had a spare dupatta and–'

'Not true, Aisha. All his idea. I just followed his instructions!' Bhabhi twisted my earlobe as my face turned pumpkin red.

'It's perfect,' said Aisha, wrapping it around her shoulders for a moment and then dropping it into the bag. 'Thank you, both of you! I have to go now!'

13

As I was getting the books out one afternoon, Bhabhi asked me to help her to make bhel. I was willing enough—I was really not in a mood to study these days—even though she gave me the nasty job of chopping onions while she blended the green-hot chutney as well as the tangy-red one. She boiled the potatoes and assembled the other ingredients, singing away tunelessly.

'Are you having guests?' I asked through my sniffles.

'No, we are going to Juhu Beach,' she said.

I almost cut myself with the knife. 'Why didn't you tell me before?'

'Because it's a surprise!'

'How are we going?'

'By auto—Sameera's dad is taking us. Aisha is coming as well!'

My heart almost stopped beating. 'Do I have time to change?'

'If you hurry with the chopping, mister!'

I chucked some onion bits at her and not to be outdone, she sprinkled some lime juice in my direction. I zigzagged my way home in a cloud of excitement, washed and changed into the red T-shirt and jeans, and got back faster than a firecracker.

Aisha stopped by the shop. She was wearing a white salwar kameez with the sparkly dupatta I'd gifted her. She didn't just look like a pari today; she was a pariyon ki rani! She told us to go ahead, her maamu and she would follow on his friend's motorbike. Today, even that information could not dim my happiness. Chachi, Sameera, Bhabhi and I piled into the auto and Chacha waved us off.

I will never forget my first glimpse of the sea. The waves, the sand, the roar—indescribable. Bhabhi pulled Sameera and me into the foamy waters. Every time the tide curled in, I leapt up with a yelp. Splashing, jumping, screaming, I couldn't have enough of it. The moist sand squished through my toes and the little crabs tickled my feet.

The sun was dipping lower and lower till it was completely sliced off by the ocean. Enough, said Bhabhi, dragging me out of the water.

Sameera wanted to build a fort and asked for my help. I was ready to build a whole city, just for the feel of those coarse grains against my skin.

Aisha and her maamu appeared a little later and Bhabhi strolled alongside them on the drier domes of sand. Chachi and Sameera's dad sat by the sugar cane juice stall.

As evening fell, Bhabhi got us to sit in a circle and play guessing games. A few rounds of antakshari were followed by the finger-licking bhel. The Maamu didn't join us. He paced up and down, gutkha in mouth, glued to his phone.

After an hour or so, in spite of our pleas, Chachi instructed us to dust ourselves off and get moving.

Aisha's dupatta flew off when she turned to wave at us on her speeding motorbike. Sameera ran and rescued it before our gang fitted ourselves back into the auto for the ride home.

Much to Bhabhi's surprise, I refused to drop the dupatta at Aisha's home. Bhabhi seemed to not realize the extent of Nani's hostility towards me. I didn't think her maamu was too fond of me either. Sameera offered to return it, so that was that.

The beach outing drew everything else out of my head for days. All I wanted to do was go back. I pestered Bhabhi every day. Not so soon, she smiled.

When Raja came by, I asked how often he went to the beach.

'Every Sunday—football followed by toddy at Marve,' he said with a wink.

I wasn't sure if I wanted to go with him, but at least I knew that option was available.

'How will the beach be in the monsoons?' I asked Bhabhi.

'Stormy and dangerous. Some of our colony boys drowned when they went swimming during the monsoons a few years ago. Don't you dare think about going!'

If only, if only, just Aisha and I could go there, build forts in the sand, get drenched, eat bhel puri and sit and talk for a whole day . . . Maybe Tiger could come along too! Wouldn't that be a fabulous day?

14

Aisha just disappeared. She had stopped coming by the shop. I found myself alone with my thoughts on the rain tree most evenings. It's like she didn't exist ever since the Maamu had arrived.

Every morning and evening, I took ten rounds of the colony on my bicycle. But still I never felt hungry. Chachi asked me what was wrong. Nothing, I said.

'He must be missing his village,' she told Chacha in a hushed tone. 'He's been away for more than a year. Why don't you talk to Sanjiv? A fortnight at home would be a good change for him. Surely you can manage without him for a few days.'

Chacha tended to his beard as he mulled over Chachi's words.

I had no desire to go back; this was my world now. But I couldn't say anything.

In the middle of some other conversation, Bhabhi said with great casualness that while Aisha's maamu was here, we couldn't expect to see much of her. Everything would be back to normal with his departure. She said we could plan another outing to the beach.

Bhabhi didn't give up trying. Nani was hobbling past the shop one afternoon when Bhabhi called out to her. 'You seem to have forgotten us, Aapa!'

'No, no, nothing like that, Sana. There's so much to do! Nadeem is here only for a few weeks, so I have to make all his favourite dishes. We shall be leaving for my sister's place in Ajmer soon. Before that we have to visit so many of our relatives. There are a few good proposals for him, but so far he has declined all the offers. Yesterday we went to Mira Road; the train was so crowded, I thought I'd faint and die! But my nephew, bless him, so concerned about me—he hired an auto on our way back.'

'That's really sweet of him! What's Aisha up to these days?'

'She's in seventh heaven, roaming all the time with her maamu. He wants her to prepare for Class X, but she refuses to touch her books this month. Now they have gone to the mall to see a movie and eat burgers! And I'm sure he's going to buy her a dress or two. He really fusses over her.'

'Tell her to show me her shopping when she's back!' said Bhabhi as the old woman continued on her way.

Bhabhi gave me a sidelong glance as if she expected this to cheer me up. I doubted very much that Aisha would ever show up.

But, wonder of wonders, she did turn up! She was dressed in a tight-fitting red outfit, in a ridiculous pair of high-heeled sandals. That too, gold with crystals.

'Bhabhi, I'm taller than you now!' she announced as she pirouetted around Bhabhi.

'That you are, Aisha! Where are you off to, with so much make-up?' Chachi asked.

'We are going for my cousin's wedding! I have to sit beside the bride, so I have to look equally good. And tomorrow we go to Ajmer for a whole week. Allah hafiz!' She tottered off on her ridiculous high heels.

Chachi and Bhabhi discussed the merits and demerits of schoolgirls dressing like grown-ups, long after she had left. I thought she looked like a red-faced baboon. And she had hardly even looked at me. That they were going away for a week did not make any difference to me. I was getting used to not seeing her even when she lived next door.

When her nani came by to share some sweets from Ajmer many days later, Chacha inquired how everything was.

'Ajmer was awfully hot; Mumbai feels like a hill station. Don't tell anyone, but Nadeem has been laid off. He has decided to remain in Mumbai and set up his business. Who can tell the future; fate may have something better planned for him?'

What news could be worse! If Nadeem was going to stay here forever, it would be the end of our friendship.

When school began in June, Aisha treaded past me on her way to school without a glance. Haughty and distant, that's how she was. Not one word! If I was in the front of the shop and she could spot me in her peripheral vision, her eyes and head would turn towards the other side or she would have something very important to whisper to her two classmates just then. The same thing would happen on the way back, every single day.

I was dying to tell her that I would be joining the Hindi-medium school. I should have started class by now, but some paperwork was taking a little longer to get sorted.

What about the afternoon Bhabhi called out her name and waved to her, urging her to drop in? I knew she had seen and heard Bhabhi, but she marched past as though she was deaf. I couldn't fathom how anyone could change so much in such a short time. She was a different person altogether!

The oddest was when I saw her with the dreaded Maamu. He would be walking ahead with chest puffed out and she following meekly a few steps behind as though she was tethered to him by an invisible rope or something. She stopped when he stopped and she walked when he did. As if nothing else mattered.

Bhabhi thought I was overreacting when I told her about Aisha's demeanour.

'I swear,' I said.

'You're just being nasty,' she said.

I threw myself into my work with all the energy and determination I could conjure up. I asked Bhabhi to teach me English. I would borrow her dictionary and books and keep reading late into the night.

Sanjiv Maama did not allow me to read inside the shack, so I would sit under the street lamp and read. Bemused with my studious ways, he said he had written to Baba that he should not be surprised if I turned into a barrister. I didn't know what a barrister was, but I knew that he was making fun of me. His sarcasm didn't dampen my resolve; if anything, it made me more determined to succeed.

15

With my nose buried in my book under the street lamp, I had become adept at filtering out the meows and bow-wows and car sounds that filled the night. But I had barely gone past the fifth page one night, when a blood-curdling whimper sliced the moist air. There was something familiar about the sound.

Flinging my book aside, I took off in search of that sound. And what I saw made me come to a horrified stop!

Raja was trying to strangle Tiger by tightening his collar. He had placed his leg on Tiger's stump, so the dog lay belly-up, trapped beneath him. Tiger had managed to scratch both his forearms before succumbing to Raja's vicious strength.

'What are you doing, Raja? What's wrong with you?'

He paid no attention to my words. Tiger squirmed and whined frantically.

'Stop it, Raja! You'll kill the poor dog!'

'That's just what I intend to do!' he muttered without taking his hands off Tiger.

I tried to get between him and the dog. He flipped me aside with one hand without loosening his grip on the collar.

My head bounced off the pole and for a moment, I was blinded. I slid slowly down to the ground, silenced, my forehead spouting blood.

The police jeep racing down the road—lights flashing, siren blazing—at that very moment must have been an act of God because nothing else could have prevented Raja from murdering the dog. In hot pursuit of who knows what, the jeep advanced inexorably.

Raja picked up the dog and hurled him across the road before jumping out of the way. Tiger gurgled and moaned before limping away into the night.

As soon as the jeep turned the corner, Raja grasped my neck with one powerful hand and shook me. I stared, terrified by his ghoulish bloodshot eyes. The nausea caused by pain and the steady drip of blood was heightened by the smell of desi liquor on his breath.

'You miserable little worm, don't you see that I can finish you off sooner than the dog?'

Ever compliant, I tried to nod, but my neck remained firmly in his grip. Abruptly, he let go of me and began sobbing, 'But what use will that be? No use.'

Seizing the pole, he cried loudly and bitterly, hitting his head against it rhythmically. My aching head hurt more to look at it, but I was in too much pain to risk talking to him. I sidled past him as fast as I could, with my palm pressed to my bleeding head. I didn't wait around to figure out the cause of his insane actions.

Just as I reached the shack, the season's first rain made its appearance, with a short but swift shower.

I told everyone that I had hurt myself doing my motorbike clean-ups; thankfully, Chacha bought my story. I did not want to encounter Raja, so I stopped going to the ashram or loitering on the road after dark.

Mercifully, Tiger showed up yapping as usual and licking me greedily, almost possessively, the day after.

'I know how you feel, brother,' I said into his ears, kissing him from head to tail.

We were doing tuitions with Bhabhi when she got a call saying her mother had had a heart attack. She left for Ratnagiri immediately.

Bhabhi would be away for two weeks, and she said that in that time, I was to be the children's sole tutor. The kids seemed to prefer me because I was eager to write their answers for them.

My confidence had grown tenfold, although my school admission was still on hold. Chachi was certain it wouldn't come through without a bribe.

The rains were taking a break after days of heavy downpours. An easy breeze carrying tiny droplets of moisture fanned me as I diced the tomatoes for the tadka. The dal simmered on the Primus.

'Gopal, are you home?'

My legs turned to jelly hearing that voice. Raja!

I kept my mouth shut and wished that there had been a hiding place or another exit. But the door was ajar, so he peeped in and entered on seeing me.

'Theek hai? Not seen you in a while.'

I carried on my work with utmost concentration. I was so nervous that I was afraid I would chop my fingers off.

'If you are busy, I'll leave,' he said.

He sounded subdued, and his swagger was largely missing. I was not completely off guard, but I looked at him and offered to make him a cup of tea.

'No, I don't want anything to drink.'

After an interminable pause, he continued, 'That night I was mad . . . with rage, with grief . . .'

I nodded.

'Stella's gone, Gopal.'

'Where?' I asked.

'I mean I've lost her. Forever. She threw the ring at me and left.'

'Why? I thought she liked you.'

'She used to. But someone snitched on me and told her stories—that my graduation certificate is fake, that I have no steady income and the motorbike belongs to my uncle. She called me a fraud and walked out.'

I nodded. I didn't dare ask him if those 'stories' were true or not.

He stepped closer. I tensed, wondering which utensil would make a good weapon, just in case.

'Shit happens, Gopal. Life is tough,' he said.

I nodded.

He walked out, shoulders drooping.

As soon as my heartbeat was near normal, I got back to seasoning the dal. I was not at all sure why he had come.

16

Nani turned up suddenly at the shop one afternoon, seeking Bhabhi's advice about Aisha's studies. Disappointed not to find Bhabhi at home, she asked Chacha to let her know as soon as Bhabhi was back.

I was no longer interested in Aisha's life, but I was still a little curious. Why was Bhabhi's help required, I wondered sourly. Surely the Maamu was the perfect guide or she could ask Aisha's schoolteachers.

Once Bhabhi was back, she got so busy that nobody remembered to tell her about Nani's visit.

A week later, Nani reappeared, looking even more distressed. Bhabhi took her into the back room to talk as I had been set to work to paint the kitchen shelves. Though they spoke in low tones, I could still hear quite a bit of what they said.

'Her teachers are very concerned about her grades. She has never performed so poorly. Nadeem sits and makes her study every day for two to three hours! I go to the park while they study so that they are undisturbed.

'Yesterday, the teacher asked the children to write an essay about their school picnic and Aisha wrote something bizarre! Nadeem was so furious that he slapped her! I told him to be gentle with her; teenaged girls have their moods. But he has so many dreams for her.

'And Sana! My little chatterbox has turned silent. She talks only when necessary. What could be wrong with her? The pressure of being in Std. X must have got to her. She may confide in you, Sana. I've brought you her books—go through them.'

Bhabhi only said 'hmm' from time to time. At the end, she promised to help in any way she could.

Aisha's falling grades didn't bother me at all. Serves her right, Ms Uppity!

After tuition, Bhabhi opened Aisha's notebook and started reading her essay aloud to me:

My school picnic

The large and friendly sun gives life to Earth. But what if it is possessed by the devil? Then it will turn dark and sinister, dripping its ash on Earth. Life, as we know it, will be destroyed. Big mighty trees will fall, rivers will run dry, birds will no longer sing and crops will rot. The human race will be vanquished! Full stop. The end.

'Has she gone mad or what?' I laughed.

My laughter didn't go well with Bhabhi. She told me I would have to come with her to Aisha's house.

'Why me?'

'Because she's your friend.'

I corrected her: 'She used to be my friend. Besides, nobody in that house likes me. And it's cloudy, it's going to rain any minute . . .'

'Come with me,' Bhabhi ordered, losing patience. 'I don't know what is happening, but something is very wrong with that child.' She told me to carry Aisha's books.

I went along sullenly. I could never refuse Bhabhi anything.

On our way, we met Nani. She had been to the doctor's and was now headed to the park as it was study time. She kissed Bhabhi's hands for taking prompt action. She did not even seem perturbed that I was also there.

The road was slippery and Bhabhi and I picked our way carefully. I was in no hurry to get to Aisha's. Half the street was taken over by a shamiana put up by Rizwan's family to celebrate his brother's first birthday. The other half had heaps of smelly rotten stuff pulled out of the drains for the delayed pre-monsoon clean-up. There was only a narrow passage for walking in between.

As we reached Aisha's house, dread was like a hard ball in my stomach. No good would come of this encounter. What was Bhabhi going to say?

I gestured to Bhabhi to take the lead. She pushed me forward instead.

I knocked on the door tentatively. Bhabhi stood behind me, on the lower step.

We heard something like a groan from inside the house. We looked at each other and listened intently.

We heard the Maamu's voice. 'Why so much fuss? Every day? You make it harder for yourself this way.'

Then there was the same stifled cry again.

And I knew. Something was terribly wrong.

I rapped loudly.

No answer.

I thumped on the door as hard as I could.

The door opened a crack.

Maamu looked at me and barked, 'What are you doing here, you filthy dog? Go away.' He started shutting the door on me.

My voice came out weak but steady, 'I've come to return Aisha's books.'

As his shoulders relaxed and he stretched his arm out for the books, I hurled myself at him, butting him in the chest to gain entry into the room. Bhabhi stumbled over him and followed in a rush.

Aisha was gagged, with her hands and legs tied to the chair she was sitting on. Her salwar and dupatta lay piled at her feet and her kameez was unbuttoned. And her unseeing eyes were fixed to the wall. Small whimpering sounds—that we had heard—came from her.

By the time Bhabhi and I reached her, Maamu had grabbed a kitchen knife from somewhere.

Slashing at me with one hand, he lunged to push me out of the house with the other. I matched him, blow for blow, and we circled the room, landing on the balcony. There was a haze in my mind—I did not know what I was doing—but I knew I had to stop this man. I don't know how long it lasted. But at one point, my hand grabbed his hand and the knife clattered to the ground. He made for the door and jumped down, on to the street.

I knew I should follow him, but I had to see if Aisha was all right.

Bhabhi had managed to free Aisha and help her get dressed. Aisha stood in that trance-like state, still making gurgling sounds. She seemed to not know we were there.

I did not know what to do. Bhabhi's eyes were filled with tears and anger.

I touched Aisha's shoulder gently. 'Aisha?'

She screeched and crumpled to the floor.

Bhabhi said urgently, 'I'll look after her. Go after the swine, Gopal. Don't let him escape!'

I could hear her calling Chacha as I sprinted down the stairs and out.

It had started raining heavily. I could see Maamu on the road, but he was far ahead of me. Though I ran as fast as I could, I did not know if I could catch up.

He was near the garbage dump, when I saw Chacha, striding towards Aisha's house. I could see the moment when Chacha noticed him.

Maamu was looking for a way over the wall. I think he was planning to cross the railway tracks and disappear. He looked once in my direction—and then he stepped straight into one of the slimy heaps of muck and fell.

By the time, I reached him, Chacha had already grabbed him.

Once the policemen had taken the Maamu away, I heard my name being called out.

'Gopal, you are bleeding,' said Sanjiv Maama, who had made a genie-like appearance.

That's the first time I noticed my shirt was blood-soaked.

Chachi and some others came, exclaiming in horror. Sanjiv Maama and Chachi threw me into Sameera's father's auto and escorted me to the hospital.

I clenched my eyes tight while they poked me and sutured me. Blood and fluids were pumped into me.

After a two-day hospital stay, I was discharged with strict orders to take bed rest. Chacha insisted that I stay with them until I had fully recovered. Sanjiv Maama agreed wholeheartedly with this arrangement.

17

I had turned into a hero. Everyone came to shake my hand. Nobody could believe that a skinny undersized boy like me was the one to fend off her maamu. I could not either.

But very few of my visitors were sympathetic towards Aisha. They did not say much to me, but I could hear them talking to Chachi and Bhabhi. They questioned her character and her upbringing. The girl thought too much of herself, they said. Surely she brought it upon herself, they said. How could Nani have been oblivious to these goings-on, they asked. The best thing would be to get Aisha married to her maamu, they concluded.

Bhabhi lashed out at these comments. She did not yell, as I felt like doing, and her voice remained calm. I could imagine her dimples flashing as she spoke. Why do you accuse Aisha of doing anything wrong, she'd say. The child is hurt and deeply traumatized; she needs our love and understanding.

I didn't see any sense in what the visitors were saying. But it still made me angry. I couldn't stand hearing anything negative about Aisha. My admiration for Bhabhi grew in these moments.

I asked everyone if I could go see Aisha, but I was told to keep away.

Bhabhi often sat with me until I fell asleep on the mattress in the kitchen. One night, she explained that it would take a long time for Aisha to be healed; she had been tortured for weeks.

'Why didn't she tell Nani?' I asked.

'Because of you,' said Bhabhi softly, ruffling my hair.

'Me?'

Bhabhi nodded. 'The scoundrel had warned her that he would harm you if she told anyone about it.'

I turned away from Bhabhi. I had doubted Aisha's friendship. She had endured so much for me. What I had done for her was just a reflex—anyone who had seen her then would have done that. But what she had done for me . . .

She was indeed my pari.

The following night, I was unable to fall asleep, though I had shut my eyes and pulled the sheet over my head. I could hear Chacha and Chachi talking in the bedroom.

'Aapa is devastated! She keeps lamenting that she was blind, that she didn't see the signs earlier. She thinks he must have had his designs on Aisha from the beginning!' said Chachi.

'Wasn't he good to Aisha when he first arrived? I remember the gifts—'

'Yes, she says that was his plan to win her. That he has been so friendly over the years. The poor girl trusted him!' cut in Chachi.

'This evil business must have begun after he lost his job.'

'Are you trying to defend him? Justify his actions?' Chachi raised her voice.

'No, of course not. I'm just trying to understand . . .' said Chacha.

'He's evil, that's all there is to it. Allah will never forgive him,' said Chachi with finality.

'I agree—but it's truly very tragic. Little Aisha, carefree and spirited, now reduced to this sad and pitiful creature. Her charm, her masti all gone!' said Chacha.

'She'll be fine, but it will take time, the doctor said,' Chachi murmured.

'How will they meet their expenses now?'

'Aapa's sister is standing by them. She's so ashamed that she's going to sell some land and deposit the money towards Aisha's education.'

'That's a fine gesture. But they mustn't withdraw the case against Nadeem,' said Chacha belligerently.

'You are right, but we can't interfere too much. After all, it's their family matter.'

This conversation kept going round and round in my head for hours.

When I finally fell asleep, an endless cycle of nightmares seized me: Aisha was walking into the sea zombielike, in spite of my shouts of warning and I couldn't do a thing! I stood by the shore, hands and feet tied while being sucked into a growing sinkhole.

18

Bhabhi, my most trusted ally, was keeping secrets from me. She had left home that morning before I awoke and she barely spoke to me after she got back in the late afternoon. Chachi stayed upstairs and Chacha stayed out in the shop. I knew they were hiding something from me.

I followed her around as she got dinner going, but she avoided all my questions. My stress grew. Something had gone very wrong.

'We have to do something for Aisha!' said the widow Martha loudly as she walked into the kitchen, followed by Tiger.

Bhabhi nodded and tried to steer her towards the bedroom.

But the widow Martha was too excited to notice. She carried on. 'The girl has gone crazy! If not for Tiger, she would have died. Aapa is shell-shocked as it is.'

I was scared to ask anything, in case she realized I was there and stopped. But my heart stood still. What had Aisha done?

'Sana, you know how tongues are wagging and people are saying all sorts of things about Aapa and her granddaughter. Who can they turn to? We have to put our heads together.'

'I know, Aunty. I have been racking my brains. That poor child needs help!' said Bhabhi. She had stopped trying to shepherd the widow Martha to the inner room. Chacha and Chachi had also come into the kitchen.

'You know my Stella is working as a counsellor in that convent school in Marve. She says she can fix up for Aisha to join the school. And Aapa can stay with her for as long as it takes; she's got staff quarters . . .'

Bhabhi broke into that big smile that had disappeared for days and her eyes shone. 'Oh Aunty, if Aapa agrees, that is such a good idea!'

'That's why I've come to you, Sana. Only you can convince them that they need to get away from this place.'

Once Bhabhi and the widow Martha left for Aisha's house, I could be quiet no longer. 'What was the widow Martha saying about Aisha? Please tell me what's going on!'

'Aisha tried to kill herself today,' Chachi sighed.

I was in shock. 'What?! Is she okay? Did her maamu reappear?'

'She's okay. Nadeem is still in police custody. But she feels very sad, very worthless. She cries all the time,' Chachi explained.

'Why? She didn't do anything wrong,' I said.

'You are absolutely right, beta. But what she went through—it changes people.'

'What did she do?' I asked hesitantly. My heart was thumping. What if she had succeeded?

Chachi told me. My heart sank when I thought of Aisha in so much turmoil. But one part of the story made me smile. 'But that was the time when Tiger comes for a biscuit every day,' said Chachi. 'Sensing something was wrong, he barked and barked until the neighbours came to see what was wrong. They broke the door down and managed to save her.'

This three-legged creature, my Tiger, was a hero!

'Are you sure Aisha is okay?'

'Yes, the dog's timing was perfect.'

When Bhabhi came back, she looked tired but happy. Aisha and her nani would be leaving for the convent the next day.

Epilogue

We reached late in the evening. I was tired, hot and sweaty. What else to expect at the beginning of November in Mumbai?

We took the bus to Malad, looking out at the roads and buildings. I still did not know very much of the city.

I had gone back home for the first time since I had come to Mumbai, some eighteen months ago. It was a short visit, but I had been excited. After Aisha left, there was a sense of sadness and I thought going home would make me feel better.

It did not, though we had gone for a celebration—well, two. Firstly, we were home for Diwali. And secondly, to Sanjiv Maama's pride and delight, my aunt was now the sarpanch. He had wanted to hire a horse for a victory ride around the village, but Baba said it was better to remain low-key; why draw attention and invite the wrath of the upper castes?

But the village did not feel like home, and maybe my home was in Squatters Colony gully.

As I sat on that bus, with the air blowing grit into my face, I thought—as I often did—of Aisha and how she was. We got some news when Bhabhi called Nani or the widow Martha's sister called her. But news was one thing and seeing her was another.

Since she had left, there was a big hole in my life.

But, I thought, there were many good things too.

Firstly, of course, there was Chacha and Chachi and Bhabhi. Chacha still paid me my full wages, though I only worked half the day. Chacha had told me I needn't work, but I pleaded with him to let me continue. I had to give up the motorbike-cleaning work, though.

Then there was Tiger. Since Aisha and Stella were gone, I had become one of his best friends. He came over to the shack every morning for some roti.

Then, there was school—I was still not sure whether that was a good thing or not. The school in the city was not that much better than the one in my village. Yes, the teachers were mostly present, but studies were still boring and tedious. Six hours at school plus hours of homework was too much, a waste of time. The only thing I enjoyed was going to the science lab, but those classes happened once a fortnight. I made sure I passed in all the subjects so that nobody would take too much notice of me. I kept telling Bhabhi that I could study with her help and appear for SSC as a private student. No, she said, you must experience school. It will grow on you, she said.

There was also Raja, busy hustling as usual. He had tied up with a local builder for the redevelopment of Squatters Colony. Residents were worried that the builder would eject them to some far-off suburb and construct brand-new towers for the wealthy. Raja was also pursuing a new love, the pujari's niece. In spite of all this, he always took me on a spin whenever he was free and to play football at Marve on Sundays.

Raja's cronies regarded me with respect now. To them I was the new toughie on the block. Yakub and Imtiaz smiled at me when we met, and the ragpickers would sometimes nod at me. Tony avoided me completely.

Best of all, though I have no idea why it happened, was that even Sanjiv Maama seemed to have changed a bit—he seemed to be trying to be friends with me. When Chacha suggested that my earnings should be deposited in the bank instead of being given to him, I thought he would be mad. But he was not. Who knew what was happening in his mind?

My evenings still ended on the branches of the rain tree. I shared the day's happenings with Tiger, who thumped his tail in answer to my utterings as he lay at the foot of the tree.

As we got off the bus near Squatters Colony, I thought maybe this was home after all.

After dropping off my bag at the shack, I went to meet Chacha, Chachi and Bhabhi. Jamirbhai had finally come to visit this Diwali, and I was looking forward to meeting him.

There was a crowd in front of the shop, looking at someone. Bhabhi was the first to see me, and she smiled and came running.

I could see the person they were looking at—sitting on my bicycle was Aisha. Her bell-like laugh rang out when she saw me.

'Guess what, Gopal,' she said. 'I have learnt to ride a bicycle. I can race you and you'll see, I will win!' She turned to Chacha. 'Chacha, I'll borrow a cycle from you. Nani is going to buy me one, but that will take time.'

'Any time,' said Chacha with a chuckle. 'I wouldn't underestimate our Gopal, but we'll celebrate whoever wins, won't we, Sana?'

'Nimbu-pani party,' said Chachi as everyone laughed.

'And Bhabhi, guess what I'm going to become?'

'Pilot,' I said, having found my voice at last.

'Not an ordinary pilot. I'm going to be an air force pilot!' she said, eyes blazing. Now that she was off the bike, I could see that she had grown taller and stronger looking.

'No, no,' said Chachi, looking horrified, 'that's too dangerous an occupation, not for girls anyway!'

'Dangerous for the enemy,' she quipped. 'I have decided and I will follow my heart.'

'Why not?' said Chacha, 'You are our bindaas girl!'

She talked and talked like only she could. I listened as I sent up prayers of thanksgiving to all the gods and goddesses for bringing my pari back.

'Aisha, we have to go home!' Nani's querulous voice broke in. I tensed up, but then I found she was looking at me with a hint of a smile. She invited Chacha and his family for lunch the following day. And then she turned to me and said, 'You too, Gopal. Come home for khatte aloo. Let's celebrate our homecoming.'

Acknowledgements

I feel privileged to express my deepest gratitude to all you amazing people:

- Dr Alice Honor Gavin, my supervisor and Dr Agnes Lehoczky, convenor of the creative writing programme at the University of Sheffield for their invaluable inputs towards this story in its nascent stage
- Sayoni Basu of Duckbill Books for displaying the best characteristics of a primary Platypus—timely nudges, infinite patience and editing genius
- Aman for the quirky and vibrant cover
- Lourdes Fernandes and Jyoti Tanna for placing me in their prayerful cocoon
- Sunita and Ramesh for goading me to 'go for it'
- Shruti, a fellow writer, chief partner-in-whining
- My string of soul sisters, A-V—Alice, Anuradha, Armin, Asha, Chitra, Fatima, Kiran, Marta, Neha, Reeta, Rekha, Sangeeta, Shashi, Shayela, Shernaz, Shilly, Vandana and Vijayam—for laughter, hugs and strong shoulders
- Mamta maushi for bhakri, poli and more
- Obelix and Evalix for avocado toast, nachos . . . Need I say more?
- Mum-dad and Rashid for filling me with their presence from the vast beyond

Zarin Virji, a creative writing graduate from the University of Sheffield, follows her passions of teaching and writing. For over three decades she has played the role of a teacher, teacher trainer and head of school. From 1996 to 2006, she edited the journal *Classroom*, a safe space for all matters related to education. Her writing is as much about expressing spontaneous feeling as it is about grappling with socio-economic realities of our times. Her poetry and short stories have been featured in publications such as *the Research Scholar*, *Route 57* and *The Best Asian Short Stories* (2018).

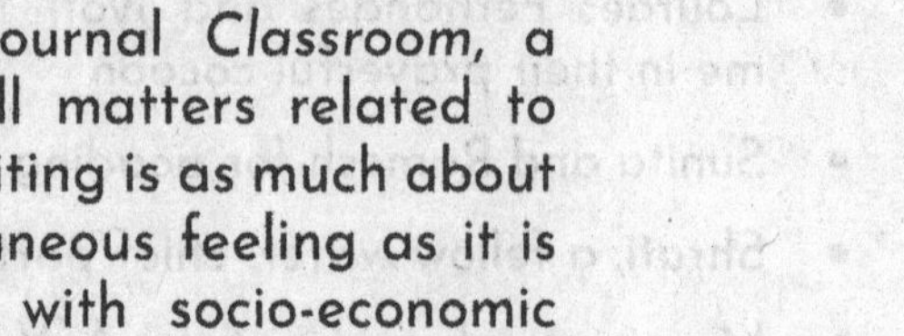